Three Changing Experiences

First Edition

Published by the Nazca Plains Corporation

Las Vegas, Nevada

2015

ISBN: 978-1-61098-387-7
E-Book: 978-1-61098-388-4

Published by:

The Nazca Plains Corporation®
Austin TX 78755

PUBLISHER'S NOTE

Three Changing Experiences is a work of fiction created wholly by Wade Wright's imagination. All characters are fictional and any resemblance to any persons living or deceased is purely by accident. No portion of this book reflects any real person or events.

Getty Images (US), Inc.
Art Director, Kimm Antell

*To each and every person on the face of the earth that has had to,
at some time in their life, make a major life changing decision.
Yes, you included!*

Three Changing Experiences

First Edition

Wade Wright

CONTENTS

The Reunion
Chapter One:
The Cute Little Sticker

"Man, I sure can't believe how just ten years ago we all talked and made remarks about how much older we'd all be when we got together for our tenth year reunion. I guess we all thought we'd all be old geezers by this time!"

"Jack, you are so right! We thought we'd have the world by the horns by this time! Well, living in fantasy was fun, I guess!"

"So Bob – didn't work out with you and Janet – I guess? Heard you guys are divorced, right? Constantly dating each other for all four high school years and always being considered the strongest of chances for the 'happily ever after couple,' just didn't follow through I guess, uh?"

"No, sure didn't! Graduation, marriage, couple of good years, then things kind of started falling apart. Really think we should have dated around a little more, I mean a hell of a lot more! We were just too much, 'B & J' as everybody said. I guess it was assumed by everybody, including us, that we were destined to be the prince and princess, have the world at our fingertips, and everything was to go off into total blissfulness forever. Well, real life just ain't like that!"

"So, Bob, any kids? I've never heard about you two having kids, but then I never asked either!"

"No, thank goodness, no! Enough of a mess in that period of my life, sure am glad no kids are involved. So – enough about me and my screwed up life! What about you? Heard you did real well in always having your name on the Dean's Honor Roll at North State, and obviously knew how to court the pretty women, too! I haven't yet met your wife, but I've been keeping my eye out for the, Miss North State Scholar and Beauty of the Year. I figured with a title like that, I'll be able to pick her out whenever I see her. I mean, well no slam to the gals from our class, but I'm sure none of them ever got a title that included the word 'beauty!' Where is she? I'm anxious to meet her?"

"Not here! Came by myself."

"What!? You did!? Uh – why didn't she come with you Jack?"

"Hey, who knows! Hey, let's get out of here and go have a couple of beers down at that ole beer hall that used to always refuse to sell to us. Now we can go in there, and buy as many beers as we want! What you say? I've about had it with this 'formal party thing!' Everybody's running around trying to look happy, and I think most of it is fake! I'm ready to get out of here, interested?"

"Yeah, I'm ready too! I've had enough 'glad hand shaking,' to last for another ten years too. Let me run over and tell Susan and Bill, or whatever her husband's name is, that I'm leaving and I'll meet you by the front door, OK?"

"Yeah, great I'll be there!"

Bob and Jack rather re-grouped when they got to the hotel's front door and then decided to just use Bob's car since they found out they were both staying there at the Central City Hotel, where the reunion was being held anyway.

As they entered the old downtown bar, Bob commented, "OK, ten years later, and sure looks like the same ole place to me! Jack, isn't that the same ole bartender that was working here, back then?"

"Sure looks like it to me! Older, but I'm sure he's the same one. Guess everybody gets older looking than we do, right?"

"Yeah, guess so!" Then slapping Jack jokingly on the shoulder, Bob added. "Well anyway, I sure do think you and I have pretty well kept our 'feline figures' up pretty well, don't you?"

Attempting to continue the joking mode, Jack looked at Bob, did a total head to toe observance and replied, "Well, for the skinny kid that couldn't keep his pants up above his crack line, yeah – I'd say you did pretty well for yourself. What'd you do, learn how to eat or something?"

As Bob ordered two, agreed upon, Buds from the bartender, paid for them and picked them up, he then held one in the air and replied, "Learned how to drink! It's all in the drinking man – all in the drinking!"

Jack rather motioned toward a corner table that was more 'out of the way' than some of the others and Bob indicated, 'head for it!'

Sitting down at the table, Jack asked, "So Bob, what went wrong? Can't imagine you and Janet not making a go of it. I did notice she wasn't there tonight, was she?"

"No, she heard I was going to be here, so she stayed away. She doesn't want to be anywhere I am. The why – too much time in the weight room, and too young to want all the 'family, married' responsibilities, that go with that funny little piece of paper."

"Oh, so the weight room is the thing that changed you, not the learning how to drink, right?"

"Na, the drinking is the result of the wanting to be out of the house! Hey – push a barbell, then go tip a Bud Better than the ole, 'Honey go empty the trash can – Honey, come help wipe the dishes – Honey, go wash the car!' "

"Well, I'm sorry the marriage thing was a bust, but if that's why you started doing the weight room thing, maybe it ended up being the better for you. Bob, you were constantly picked on in school since you didn't have any butt on you and your pants kept trying to fall off, but I'm not blind and once I realized who in the hell you were tonight, I was shocked! You've done good for yourself, well anyway build wise. You look good! Really!"

"Well thanks man, thanks! Always nice to have someone say good things about yourself. Thanks! So, the big why! Why you here, all alone, when it is the perfect time to show off the beauty? I'm sure everybody in that class is wondering right now, just where is she? I know Susan and Kathy were talking back at the table, and they were trying to watch you, to see where she, as they referred to her as – where 'she' was."

"Hey, man, when I found out from you, that you and Janet didn't make it, that's when I decided you were the right guy for me to go do some good ole drinkin' with. My life is shit too! Marilyn and I are separated. What can I say, happens to all of us I guess!"

"Oh shit man, I'm sorry! Jack, I'm sorry to hear that! I know the crap you are going through! I really do. Want to talk about it? Don't have the ole psychology degree, but sure do have the personal experience. Maybe I can help you, some way!"

"Hey – don't think anybody can help me much! Just not in the mood to be married anymore! Once we got out of college, life was beautiful and of course, my Mom and Dad, and her Mom and Dad kept throwing too much at us, trips and things, like expensive gifts, and after a few years of that, I guess I just decided I had everything but obviously not what I really wanted!"

"Uh – like what was it you really wanted? What was that?"

"I don't know! I really don't! Just some loving, I guess! Not so much 'stuff' and all that primp and proper high class living – just some good old down to earth living and loving!"

"So, where you stand? Like – what's up? You guys divorced or just separated, or what?"

"Hell, I don't know. No, yeah – I mean, no we're not divorced, but I'm not living there. I took a small apartment in Philly."

"So, like you seeing anyone, or how's the 'getting the loving' going that you need?"

"Hey man, guess maybe we need to get onto something else! Maybe talking love life is not so easy for me. Hey – let's talk about you guys. What happened with you and Janet?"

"Well, like you just said, talking is pretty hard when the questions are straight forward. All I can say is, we weren't like we thought we were. I mean, hey, we grew up and started realizing new stuff."

"Bob, straight question – you realized what? You realized what?"

"Oh crap man, crap. Personal stuff, I guess. Just stuff that didn't work out so well in the married life! That's all."

"Fooling around with some other gal?"

"No, hell no! No, I wasn't fooling around with some other gal!"

"Some other guy?"

"Jack, how in the hell can you ask that? Why in the hell would you ask that?"

"Well man, your answer, 'No, I wasn't fooling around with some other gal.' I just kind of felt like there was a little too much emphasis on the word gal! You didn't just say you weren't fooling around. You stated a gal!"

"Well fucking shit man, just because of the way I said that, it makes me a gay or something?"

"Well, let's just say that, and the cute little sticker you got on the back of your car!"

"Oh shit man! Oh crap! Oh Jack, I totally forgot about that. Uhhhh – I kind of guess then, that you know what a Leatherman's gay sticker looks like then, right? I mean, well – hell yeah, I guess you do, don't you?"

"Yeah – yeah. Bob, I got vibes about you back at the banquet hall, especially once I saw that new body of yours, and then when we went into the parking garage and I walked up behind the Monte Carlo that you said was yours, then I knew for sure! I know, everybody's not supposed to know what that is, but hey man – I do. I've seen 'em. There used to be a gay club close to the college dorm I lived in, and I finally found out what all those little stickers meant. Never went there, but I do know. And Bob, your life style is O.K. with me. Everybody's not the same, and I've got some gay guys working for me at the company, so don't freak out and think I'm going to have a problem with it! OK?"

With Jack's admission that he now knew a little more about Bob and why he and Janet had separated, the conversation became much more open and comfortable. For hours, the two former classmates discussed a multitude of topics, some old, and some new. Some good stuff and some pretty down stuff. They each had a number of times to console each other and promise 'better days ahead.' Not only did they talk, they also drank! Boy, did they drink!

They agreed that they were finally making up for all of the times when the bar would not sell to them because they were too young.

Hours later, the bartender approached and said, "Men, it's closing time. Where you two have to go to? Neither one of you are in any kind of shape for driving. I'm going to call you a cab, OK?"

Bob looked at Jack and then at the bartender that had come to their table, and replied, "O.K. man. Yeah. Yeah – do that! Hell man, got to admit right now, I'm not sure I'd remember how to get back to the ole hotel anyway."

The bartender called the cab, it arrived, and the two friends that definitely became much closer during the past five or six hours, arrived at the hotel.

As the cab drove off, Jack turned to Bob and said, "Shit man. I hope like hell nobody else is still up. I'd hate like hell for them to see us as shitting assed drunk as we must be."

Bob looked at Jack, and agreed. "Hey, all I can say is, thank goodness for elevators or I'd be sleeping on the lobby floor. Three steps would be three steps too many for me right now."

Getting into the elevator, Jack hit floor four, and Bob stood there stupidly and looked at Jack and said. "Shit man, what floor am I on? Jack – I can't remember what floor my room is on."

"Oh hell man, don't worry!" Jack replied. "Hey just come to my room till you remember!"

As the elevator stopped at floor four, Bob was still trying to find his room key so he could remember where his room was, but he could not find it.

"Hey don't worry man, don't worry! Let's just go to my room and worry about that after we get some sleep. We both need to hit the hay real bad!"

"Oh shit Jack! I know where it is! I put it in the seat thing in my car. Oh shit man, the car's at the bar! Oh shit!"

Both men were definitely feeling the sorrows of not only beer – a few or more, but plus some shots of some stronger strengths.

"Hey man, don't worry! We'll get it tomorrow. We need to do some sleeping first, though!" Jack replied. "Come on man, here's my room."

Bob and Jack went into Jack's room, and Bob immediately fell across the double bed in the room.

"Hey man, get undressed! Don't go to sleep there all dressed. You've got to wear those clothes tomorrow until we get your car and get your room key."

Bob attempted to get up to get undressed, but in his state of 'one or two too many,' he kept falling back down and landing across the bed.

"Come here man, let me help you!" Jack said as he grabbed Bob and started to help him get undressed. He was successful in getting his shoes and shirt off, but since Bob kept sitting down, he did have some trouble getting his slacks off. Finally he laid Bob down across the bed, and managed to pull his slacks off. He did not attempt to remove Bob's briefs, but much to Jack's surprise, that did seem to be the one item that Bob did know he did not want to have on.

The Reunion
Chapter Two:
Let Me Hug You

"I never wear underwear when I'm in bed!" Bob managed to get out, in a very stuttering fashion, as he, himself, did manage to get his Jockeys pulled off.

Jack finished getting undressed and after managing to get Bob moved over in the bed, and headed the right direction, Jack laid down beside him. Much to his complete surprise, Bob slightly, and slowly moved over toward him and put his right arm across his chest. Not knowing exactly what he should do, Jack just laid there.

"Come here man, let me hug you!" Bob quietly said. "You need some huggings."

"Bob, please, I don't think we should be doing this. Let me just lie here and go to sleep, OK?"

"Come on Jack! Relax! Nothing bad's gonna happen! Just let me hug you some. You need it!"

Jack didn't fight back, but he was rather uncomfortable with Bob wanting to hug, but Bob was rather insistent and did not stop.

Bob continued to hug Jack's chest and managed to pull him even a little closer. "Come on man. I remember what we talked about back at the bar, your life's been crap lately, you need some hugging."

"Well yeah, I will admit to that, but Bob, you're the gay guy, I'm the straight guy, and I'm not so sure I can get into what I guess maybe you're wanting to do."

"Hey man. All I want to do is let you know somebody loves you man, just somebody loves you. From what you told me, I'm not too sure you know that anymore!"

"Yeah Bob, I don't! She's been such a bitch to me lately, you are right, I don't think anybody does love me anymore!"

"Yes we do man, yes we do. Let me hug you. It's just one body up against another body, nothing wrong with two people being close to each other!"

Jack rather did accept what his rather drunken friend was managing to talk about, and he did start to relax and just let Bob squeeze him. Jack did realize that it was just two human bodies up against each other, and there shouldn't be anything wrong with that.

Bob snuggled up closer and silently continued to hug Jack, as he also placed his face up against Jack's shoulder. He could tell Jack was starting to accept the touching and feeling, and he even thought that perhaps Jack was actually enjoying it.

For quite some time, twenty or twenty-five minutes, the two men laid there and Jack allowed Bob to hug him, squeeze him, and even move his hand around some on his upper body. For some initial times as Bob's hand moved around, Jack got a little tense, but then he finally started to relax again and allow Bob to roam some more. Finally Bob's hand reached the top of Jack's briefs. Very slowly Bob slid his middle finger under the elastic band of the briefs and felt Jack take a deep breath. Jack did not say anything, nor did Bob. Realizing that Jack was not openly objecting to his actions, Bob decided to see just how far down into those briefs he could put his hand. Slowly and carefully Bob extended his reach, and shortly could feel the tips of his fingers touching Jack's cock.

"Uh, Bob, stop! Bob please!"

"Hey man, lie still. Everything's OK. Nothing's wrong! Let me just feel you, OK?"

"Bob you are feeling me man! You are!"

"I know and you feel good! Jack, you need this attention man, you need someone caressing you and feeling you. Jack you told me back at the bar that it's been four months since you and Marilyn have done anything. You need some good ole touching. If I touch it, it ain't gonna fall off or anything! Come on man, relax!"

Bob managed to slide his hand down in farther, into Jack's briefs, and he did take hold of Jack's soft meat. "See man, my touching it ain't hurt'en any, is it?"

Jack did not respond, but Bob could feel him rather adjust as if to get more comfortable lying there!

Bob turned over more toward Jack and with one hand in Jack's briefs, he then reached up and with his other hand, massaged Jack's shoulder. "Relax man, relax!" He stated and encouraged. "Jack your muscles are stiff as a board. You're OK. You need to try and relax. Come on man, lie on top of me."

Bob slid over so that he could lie completely flat on his stomach and again he encouraged Jack to lie on top of him.

"Come on Jack. You will be fucking surprised at how lying on top of another person and just letting your body go can be so relaxing and can feel so good. Come on man, nothing bad is gonna happen. Just get up on my back and lie down on me. Let your body feel me and my warm body. You'll be surprised at how good that feels."

"Hey Bob, you're drunk man, you're drunk. Let's just go to sleep. OK?"

"No, no! No Jack, I'm not that damn drunk! I know what I am talking about. I've known ever since back at the bar how up tight you are about everything going on in your life right now, and from experience, I know what it feels like to just let your body lie on top of another good warm body. Jack, I'll just be lying here, arms stretched up by my head. You just lie down on top of me, and relax. Come on man, come on!"

Jack finally decided that maybe Bob did kind of know what he was talking about, and he slowly repositioned himself so that he was lying on Bob's back.

"Now just lie there and relax. Let your body feel mine!"

"Yeah, but Bob, ain't I kind of heavy lying on top of you like this?"

"No Jack, no you are fine. Really man, this feels as good for me as it does for you! Relax man, relax!"

Jack finally accepted that what he was now doing was in fact a good thing, and he was starting to feel the relaxing effects that Bob had so strongly encouraged him to accept. "Yeah Bob, I will admit, this is good! Just don't ever tell anybody that I laid on top of you when you didn't have anything on, but yeah, this is feeling good. I was all up tight and tense wasn't I?"

"Yeah you were! I kept hoping back at the bar that the drinks would kind of relax you some, but I think the more you talked about you and Marilyn, the more tense you got. Feeling better?"

"Yeah, yeah I guess so."

"Good, I knew damn well you would if I could only talk you into it!"

Bob could tell, as he simply laid there and did not make any moves, that Jack was definitely accepting the good relaxing effect of lying on his bare body. He could feel Jack slightly move back and forth once in awhile, and he could tell that Jack was attempting to feel all available areas of Bob's body up against his own.

"You all relaxed now? You feeling O.K. with this?" Bob asked.

"Yeah, I am. I know I was pretty up tight about doing this at first, but now that I've been lying here, it's good. Real good!"

"Good! Jack – take your shorts off! Really man, you think this feels good, you take you shorts off and let the rest of your skin touch mine and then you will really find out how great body to body contact can be. Hey, stop and think about it. How longs it been since you and Marilyn just laid in bed and just let your bodies touch each other? I know how married life is, in bed, slam bang thank you ma'am, and then to your own side of the bed and asleep. Hey, used to be there. I remember! Boy – do I remember!"

"OK, you finally proved this feels good, but just keep your hands up there and don't you go reaching back here and trying to grab my dick or anything! OK?"

"Yeah OK! I won't grab your dick or anything. Just take your shorts off and lie back down. Honestly, you will be damn glad you did."

Jack did slide his shorts off, and then laid back down across Bob's body. He attempted to pull his dick to the side so that it was not directly on Bob's ass crack. Bob could feel him positioning himself on his back.

"There, just lie there and relax. Kind of put your arms around my chest and hang on! Yeah – there – comfortable?"

"Yeah – got to admit – you sure do know the relaxing techniques! Bob this does feel good! Shit man, I will have to admit, you knew what you were talking about! I never in my wildest dreams ever thought I'd find, lying with a man under me, was going to be a way to make me relax. Shit man, it works!"

Bob was very patient with letting Jack completely relax by lying on top of him, and he did not say anything for quite some time. He wanted Jack to totally accept the relaxed feelings that he knew Jack was now experiencing. Occasionally Bob could feel Jack slightly move and readjust how he was lying. He also could feel Jack's cock starting to stiffen and move about. He wondered if Jack was conscious of what was happening.

"Hey Jack, just stick that thing down in between the cheeks of my butt. You can lie down on me flatter that way."

Without saying anything, much to Bob's surprise, Jack did. Without any objections that Bob expected to hear, Jack raised up enough to take his man stick, his now rather firm man stick, and he poked it down between Bob's ass cheeks as Bob slightly moved his legs apart so as to give it a place to land, and then moved his legs back together, and so slightly gripped the tool, in-between both legs. Jack laid back down, and re-gripped Bob's chest. He slightly hugged.

"You OK?" Bob asked.

"Yeah, I am – I am, but Bob, I've got to admit that I know I've gotten a hard-on lying here, and I'm not so sure I should have. Bob, you're a guy! I'm lying on top of you, and now I've got a hard-on. I'm not so sure this is all OK!"

"Why? So what in the hell is so wrong with having a hard-on? You finally got relaxed enough so that you're not all up tight with everything in life! Enjoy it man, enjoy it!"

"Enjoy what man? Enjoy what? The fact that I've got a hard-on stuck down between your bare legs, or enjoy life? What you talking about? Bob, how in the hell can I enjoy the fact that I'm lying here, completely naked, on top of you, completely naked, and now I've got a hard-on stuck down between your legs? Bob, I'm not gay! I know you are, and that's O.K. with me. I don't have a problem with that, but Bob, I'm straight! I shouldn't have a hard-on! Hell man, I really shouldn't be lying here all naked with another, all naked guy!"

"Hey man, relax! It's just you and me! If you think you shouldn't have a hard-on lying here like this, then you think you should be dead! Jack, you're human! Let yourself enjoy whatever is happening at the time. Right now your body is feeling good being up against another person's body, and your dick is just telling you that! So big deal if it's hard! Be glad it can get hard! You'd be plenty pissed if it didn't get hard, right?"

"Yeah, I know, but straight guys are not supposed to get hard when they feel some other guy!"

"So you are saying what?"

"What you mean? What am I saying, what you mean?"

"Jack, relax! Lie still! Let me enjoy the feeling of you lying there! If your dick is hard or not, is no big deal! If it feels good to me, then let me enjoy feeling it!"

Jack and Bob did lie there, with of course Jack on top, and Bob realizing that more and more, he was feeling Jack's mid torso move a little more and more.

Finally Bob said, "I want you to fuck me!"

"What!? What? Bob, no, I can't do that! Bob! I can't!"

"And the reason you can't – is?"

"Bob we're both still drunk! I'd be sorry tomorrow! Bob, I can't! I know for you, it's no big deal, you probably get fucked by guys all the time, but Bob, I don't fuck guys!"

"So tonight, you do! Jack, I have been feeling that rod of yours sweeping back and forth across my ass, I've felt it going up and down in-between my legs, you've practically jacked it off using my legs. Admit it man, admit it. You're more anxious to let it slide up in my ass and get rid of those juices, more than I am for you to fuck me! Admit it Jack, you want to see what a guy's ass is like, right?"

"Oh God Bob, oh God! Oh shit man! Oh Bob – yeah I guess maybe I do, but Bob, if I fuck you, then – oh what in the hell am I trying to say? Oh shit man, yeah – you are right. Yeah I want to find out what a guy's ass is like – but Bob – – – – – -!"

"O.K. so – but Bob – what? But Bob, if I fuck your ass, then I'm gay? Is that what you're asking? So who in the hell fucking cares? Maybe this will be the only time you fuck a guy's ass, and hey – maybe it will only be the first time of many, many more fucks! God Jack, do it once and find out! You are just like every other boy that grows up. Every boy, regardless of what he says, wants to know what it is like to poke some other guy in the ass. You've got the chance! Hell man, you already earlier tonight made a comment about how nice my butt looks now. Hell man, you even said that before you found out I am gay! Come on Jack, let loose and do something out of the norm for a change. Hey, coming from the family you did, I'd be surprised if you ever did anything except what Mommy and Daddy told you to do. Hell, you probably did everything Marilyn told you to do too! Right? Ever do anything just for yourself?"

"Oh shit man! Oh shit! Oh God Bob, if I do – I mean, well, what if I like it? What if I fuck your ass and then find out I like doing it? Then what?"

"Then what, what?" Rather laughing, Bob answered, "Well, then we will get some sleep, and then wake up in the morning and you will fuck me again! OK?"

"Oh Bob, that's what I'm afraid of. Bob, I'm afraid I might like it and will want to do it again!"

"So fucking big deal! So you like it. If you like it, what's the big deal? Maybe that's the real reason things between you and Marilyn didn't work out so well. Maybe you need to find out for sure just what makes that dick of yours happy. Hey man, took me a while but I finally found out what was wrong, and I finally admitted that I liked a good strong solid body in bed with me instead of some fluffy female body. Yeah – I still love Janet, but she's a gal, and I like fucking around with guys. When I'm fucking something I want to feel some good strong solid muscles in it! Maybe you are the same, and maybe you aren't. But Jack, let me tell you one thing right now. Until you do it once, you will never know! I think you already have an idea you are going to like it, and since Mommy and Daddy have not told you to go do it, you're afraid to do it, right?"

"Fuck man, give me your fucking ass! I am going to find out! For once I will do something that I want to do and not ask Mommy and Daddy if I can do it! Shit – they're the ones that even picked Marilyn out for me! My whole fucking life has been doing what Mommy and Daddy wanted me to do, and I am fucking tired of it! I am going to fuck your ass and I am going to enjoy it! And the whole time I'm fucking your ass I'm going to be yelling, 'Mommy watch me fuck his ass, watch me fuck his ass!' "

"Now you're talking man, now you're talking! Jack, spit some spit right onto my hole, and wet it up some, then aim your rod right in there and fuck me man, fuck me!"

Jack took the instructions to heart and got himself ready for his first man butt fuck. He aimed his hard-on right at Bob's butthole and started pushing. "Is this going to hurt you any?" He asked of Bob.

"No, not really. If you push in too fast it probably will since my ass isn't opened yet, but believe me man, once you are up in there, it's going to be all pleasure. How you doing? You doing OK?"

"Oh yeah man, I'm doing fine. I sure as the hell never expected something like this to happen while here at the reunion, but man, I've got to tell you I sure don't have any regrets over it. Bob, I've wondered for a hell of a long time just what it would be like to butt fuck some guy, but I never had the nerve to find some guy I could do it with. This is good! Your ass is tight, isn't it? I mean, I can really feel your butt muscles grabbing on my dick. I've never had my dick stuck in anything like this that feels that tight on it. Man, I bet when I shoot, I'll shoot like a fucking cannon. Man it feels tight!"

"Yeah, it feels tight, and it feels good! I didn't look at your dick once it got hard, but from what I'm feeling back there, it must be pretty good sized. It sure is feeling good in me. You got it all the way in?"

"No. No, I've only got probably half of it up in you. You want me to push it in farther?"

"Oh hell yeah man! Yeah – push the whole thing up in me. Let me feel it, all of it!"

Jack did as Bob had asked, and as he hit the end of it, he told Bob, "Oh man! What a fucking feeling! Oh man this feels so good! You OK? I've got all of my dick up in your ass now. You OK?"

"Oh fuck yes, I'm O.K. man! Fuck my ass good and hard now. Jack, you're fucking a guy now, and a guy likes to get it good and hard and rammed really rough. Do me, man, do me! Fuck me like some wild animal!"

"You sure? Bob you sure you want me fucking you hard and ramming your ass like that? Isn't that gonna hurt? Bob, I'm serious, I don't want to hurt you any. You sure?"

"I am fucking sure man, fucking sure! There ain't no reason to get fucked in the ass unless it's good and rough! Ram my ass and ram me good!"

"Bob, are you sure? Have you been fucked real hard like that before? Remember you've had a lot to drink tonight and maybe that's the reason you think you want it rough!"

"Jack believe me, it's not the alcohol, it's the dick in my ass. You have no idea how fucking great this is to have some guy lying on your back with his dick stuck up in your ass and then having him use your ass like a fucking steam roller going down the street. Don't worry about me and my ass. Fuck me like you've never fucked anything before and let your rocks fly. Believe me man, you will be damn glad you did. Just close your eyes and make believe your dick is a jack hammer and let it work on my ass like it's breaking up some concrete. Fuck it hard and fast! Now shut the hell up and fuck the hell out of my ass!"

Jack finally heard what Bob was saying and he finally gave up worrying about if he was going to hurt Bob and his ass any. Using Bob's suggestion of thinking of his dick as a jack hammer, Jack grabbed hold of Bob around the chest and started the ramming that Bob had been begging for.

"Oh my God Bob, oh my God! Oh man, I've never felt anything like this before. Oh Bob – you OK? Oh shit man this feels so good! Oh Bob, how in the hell can you take this? Oh my dick's never felt this good! Oh it feels like it's about to explode! Oh Bob, I've never had a hard-on this fucking big before! Man, it is stretched! I mean really stretched! Man it feels so fucking big! Oh I never knew fucking some guy's ass could feel this fucking good! Oh man, I'm about wiped out. Shit man, this is fucking good! Bob, you OK? You OK?"

"Oh yeaaaah – I'm more than OK, I'm in fucking heaven. Jack, I am so fucking glad this is happening. Man, for a guy that's never fucked an ass before, man alive, you sure as hell can fuck! Man, I haven't been fucked like this for a hell of a long time. Fuck me man fuck me! Let me get your juices man! Let me feel you hit my guts up in there! Load me! Shoot your rocks off so I can feel it! Oh Jack, grab me, squeeze me man, fuck me, load me, let me feel you! Yeah – yeah hug me tight!"

"Oh Bob – Bob – I'm gonna cum man, I'm about ready to cum!!! Oh man, oh man here it comes – I'mmmm cummmmin man – I'mmmm cummmin! Oh shit Bob, I just drained it man – I came like a fucking race horse! Oh Bob, I shot all my cum up in your ass! Oh man, I'm drained. That fucking wore me out! Oh Bob what an experience! Oh shit man! Now I know what I've been missing in my life! Shit I wish you and I had done this a long time ago. Bob, how did you get your first fuck? How long you been doing the gay stuff?"

Feeling completely exhausted and weak, Jack just laid down across, and still in Bob, as he attempted to regain some strength after unloading all of his energy and male juices up, and in, Bob's ass. As he attempted to relax there, he questioned Bob about how he had gotten started doing what Jack now realized was the one thing he has been missing in his life.

"Jack, it happened all by what I like to call an accident, but really I do think there was a little more unconscious planning to it than I ever admitted."

"What? What do you mean, unconscious planning? What's that mean?"

"What I mean is, I really do think I was trying to get a chance to have me and some guy do something, and at that time I really wasn't so sure of just what, but unconsciously, I was always trying to have, or make, something happen. Well, one day, it finally did! Brad – one of my co-workers at the time – we finally did it."

The Reunion
Chapter Three:
I Fucked His Ass!

"Did it? What did you do? You did what?"

"The same thing you and I just did! I fucked his ass! He sure didn't beg for me to fuck him good and rough like I had to with you, but none the less, I finally fucked him, and when I was done, I knew I had fucked him good. It was a year or so after school. I was working for Stanley Construction Company, doing some basic framing. Brad was about twenty-five or twenty-six, and of course I was only about, what, nineteen at that time? Brad was a pretty boy, so to say. He was built and he knew it, but he never acted all stuck up over it! He had muscles and he let 'em show whenever he could. Well, in the summer, his normal attire was always cut offs and tank tops! Looked like a million dollars, too! Hell, I watched a lot of people take a second look at him whenever they saw him dressed like that! He was the reason I started the gym workouts. Fact is, he was like my coach and my instructor for a while when I was getting started."

"Anyway, one Friday afternoon he and I were the last two guys on the site. All the other guys had left for the day, and Brad and I were still doing some framing. We wanted to get one small section done so that it was good and sturdy. Anyway, Brad was up on the ladder and I was down below! I was down below, and looking up. Kind of like some little kid looking up in some gal's dress. He looked down and saw me looking up the legs of his cutoffs. He smiled at me – once I kind of 'came to' – and I realized that he was standing there and watching me look up his cutoffs. He just looked, smiled and the said, 'Hey we can do something about that just as soon as I finish hammering this in place!' "

"Oh shit man, weren't you all embarrassed? Didn't that embarrass you?"

"Yes, hell yes it did! But at the same time, I wanted to find out what he meant by his comment, 'We can do something about that.' That comment made me breathe real hard, and I actually started to get a hard-on, which he mentioned. He was up there looking down at me and said, 'Hey! Thank goodness it's just you and me here now. Look at that tent you're showing!' I looked down and just about fainted when I saw the big boner that I was showing. Really until he mentioned it, I did not know it was showing like that. I really didn't!"

"God man, that had to be weird. Was this Brad guy gay, or was he a straight guy?"

"He was as gay as a pink door knob, but he was married. Hell, I always kind of figured that if his wife knew what he was doing outside of the bedroom, she was just putting up with it just so she could have her turn at him whenever he was home. Seriously, he was that fucking hot! Course, got to remember she couldn't fuck his ass, which he definitely loved, so maybe she just knew that he needed that and she let him do the guy thing to get his ass fucked once in awhile. I never asked! Believe me, I sure didn't want to do anything that would mess up my action with him."

"Oh God Bob, I can't believe this! You and Janet were married at that time, weren't you? You guys got married right after getting out of school didn't you?"

"Yeah we did. Yeah, I was married, he was married! Two married guys doing each other was heaven. What a fucking turn-on knowing that we each had women back home waiting for us, and we're hiding out fucking each other!"

"Oh he fucked you too? I mean, you fucked him and he fucked you too?"

"Oh yeah! Oh yeah! Yeah he fucked like a king! Yeah, he wanted guys to fuck his ass, but he sure did not have any problem giving it back to them. Whenever we got together, first he'd want me to fuck his ass, then when I got done, he'd always throw me over and immediately slam into me like there was a big emergency. I think he kind of always felt like if he didn't get it up in me pretty fast, then he was going to be shooting it across the floor, and he always wanted to know some guy got it. I think it was kind of his ego thing. He always wanted to know the other guy was leaving with some of him, up inside of the guy's ass."

"Man, this is great! Bob, this is making me hard again. Is it O.K. if I keep fucking your ass while you tell me about that Brad and you? This OK?"

"Hell yes it's OK. Feels fucking good! If you get all excited again, fuck the hell out of me! I'll never tell you to stop. Once I get a dick up in there, I want it to stay just as long as possible!"

"OK, I'll fuck you, while you tell me about you and Brad fucking each other, OK? Hey, get back to that first time. He's up on the ladder and you're looking up at him, what happened?"

"Oh yeah, yeah. Well, he's up on the ladder and he told me to steady the ladder and don't let it slip. He wanted me to stay right there where I was. He said, 'Make sure I don't fall.' Hell man, he was only about four or five feet off the floor, and there was no way in hell he was going to fall from that height. With me standing there, my face was almost right at his ass line the way it was. Anyway, after he told me to steady the ladder, then he reached inside of his cutoffs and pulled his dick out of the jock strap he had on. He looked back down at me and again said, 'Make sure I don't fall.' Oh man, when he pulled that dick out, I almost fainted. What a beautiful dick! He knew it and he wanted to show it off. When he pulled it out of the strap, it almost came out of the bottom of his shorts! Soft it was probably five inches long, and when it got hard, it doubled, I swear! I never did measure it, but fuck it was one fucking big dick! God did it feel good up in my ass! Hell that's the reason I think his wife didn't make a fuss about him fucking around with me or any of the other guys. She wanted that dick up in her as much as we wanted it up in us!"

"My God man, how many guys was he playing with?"

"Oh – he had a lot! I don't know for sure just how many, but when you've got a body like he had, and a dick like he had, hell I'm surprised that he didn't play with someone twenty-four hours a day!"

"Shit man, I guess he did sound like a 'hotty,' as I guess they say. So anyway, he's got his dick hanging out for you, what'd you do?"

"Oh, yeah. Well, I was standing there with my face probably only about three feet away from it, and he kept putting his hand in his shorts and pushing it down his leg. Then he'd always say, 'Don't let me fall. Hang onto the ladder!' Hell he wasn't going to fall, he wanted me standing there and looking at his rod. He knew damn well that he was really playing games with my mind, and he knew damn well that I wanted to do stuff with him and that dick. Well anyway, after about five minutes of this, he finally came back down off of the ladder and actually walked right up to me and grabbed my dick. He looked at me and said, 'Everybody needs a chance to see what it's like, and I know you are real anxious to find out. Come on, let's go have a beer in my camper.' He had one of these cab over campers on a pickup truck, and he just didn't have any second guesses about if I was willing or not. I guess for him, everybody just does it! I really don't know if any guy ever turned him down or not! Hell, I had been dreaming about doing this ever since he first came on the job about four months earlier, so I sure as hell was not going to object."

"We picked up stuff and went over to his camper. He did have some beer in the refrigerator in there, so he got one out for each of us, and then he just very casually took off all of his clothes. I just kind of sat there on the seat and watched, and then he said, 'Well, come on man. Let me see what you've got! Come on, take it off!' I felt real weird, but there was no way in hell was I going to object. I took everything off, and he grabbed my dick, which was, of course, hard, and he said something like, 'Nice dick. Your body needs some meat on it, but hell man, your dick sure will work.' Then he just took a tube of KY, put some up in his ass and said, 'Fuck me!' I had to tell him I had never fucked some guy before and he just said, 'My asshole is back there, you'll figure it out.' And then he just laid there. Laid there as if we did this together all the time. I got up on his ass and not knowing for sure what in the hell I was doing, I pointed my dick at his asshole and I pushed it in. I pushed it all the way in. I guess maybe I pushed in a little too fast since he almost screamed. Then he said, 'Oh God man! I guess you haven't fucked some guy before have you? God man, with a dick like that, you need to go a little slower until you get the guy open. Hey, don't worry. You're in now, and the pain quit, so now let me feel you up in there! Fuck me and fuck me like a champ!' "

"Oh fucking shit man, fucking shit! I can't believe this! Oh Bob, what an experience! You just pointed it and slammed your whole fucking dick up in him, all at once? Shit man, that has got my dick pumping. Oh I'm going to fuck you some more, OK?"

"Hell yeah man! Yeah – fuck me as much as you want! I'll be Brad, and you be me, and fuck me like I fucked Brad that day in his camper!"

Trying to fuck Bob's ass as fast and as hard as he could, and at the same time hear what Bob's first time was like, was really keeping things busy. "Oh man, I can't believe this! Oh Bob I can't believe I'm fucking the hell out of your ass while you're telling me about how you fucked the hell out of that Brad guy and his ass. So tell me, keep it up, tell me what happened then? Oh man I'm so hot! This is more fucking fun than I've had in years!"

"He told me to fuck him good and hard, and I did! Hell man, I had never been in another guy's ass before, and when he said to fuck him hard, I did. I fucking wore myself out. I shot more cum up in his ass, on that one shot, than I think I had ever shot, all added together before. I guess he could really feel it when I loaded him too, cause he kept yelling 'Yeah man, yeah man! Load me man, load me!' That was the first time I had ever had someone yelling at me to let my load fly and to keep it up! I guess it was really hitting him good and hard, cause he kept begging for more. Shit man, I was dry! I had drained all of it up in him. His ass had to be full of cum. I felt like I had dumped about a quart of juices up in his ass. Once I got done dumping, I collapsed on him. I was fucking exhausted! I thought I had fucked pretty well before, but man – that was the greatest fuck I had ever done. I knew right then that the man-fuck was the real way to fuck. Sex with Janet after that was never right. Every time I fucked her, I wanted to be fucking Brad instead! Hell – couple of times, I even almost called her Brad when I was climaxing."

"Oh my God Bob, you never did, did you? Oh God man, I hope like hell you never called her Brad."

"No, I never did, but I sure was dreaming about him while I was doing her."

"Oh man, I'm glad you didn't call her that! Shit man, thank goodness you never did that! So tell me man, tell me, after you dumped everything up in Brad, then what happened?"

Getting his own ass fucked good and hard, and fast as a jack hammer, was creating a real problem for Bob to do much talking, but he was smart enough to know that his comments and descriptions of his sex with Brad was one of the things that was making Jack an outrageous horny and active cock top, and he decided that he'd keep talking just as long as possible, if it meant that doing so would keep Jack wild and horny for fucking his ass, as roughly as he was now doing.

"Hey, when I fell down on his body from exhaustion is when, all of a sudden, he told me he wanted to fuck me! I thought, oh shit man, he wants to put that big long pole of his up in my ass! It scared the fucking hell out of me! His pole was enormous, and right then the idea of that thing going up in me scared the shitting crap out of me. I wasn't so sure that was going to work. I told Brad I thought I really wanted fucked, but I didn't think maybe by him. I liked him a lot, but God, putting that big thing up in me for my first fucking, I wasn't sure!"

"Oh God man, tell me, tell me! Oh man, I'm about ready to cum in you again! Oh Bob, I'm about ready to dump another load in you! Oh man, did he fuck you?"

"Oh hell yes he did! He pulled out from under me, took a hold of me and laid me down on my gut on the bed, and with me shaking like hell, he got on my butt. I felt some KY lube going up in my ass. I guess he just put the tube at my butthole and squeezed the tube and shot some, well – really quite a lot, up in me. Then the next thing I knew, I felt his dick head right at my cherry hole. Oh man I wanted to fucking scream for help. I knew what he acted like when I poked his hole, and my dick is not nearly as big as his, and besides he was used to having some guy stick his dick up in there, so I was fucking scared. I mean, really scared! Oh God Jack – you're cummmmin man – your cummin! I can feel you dumping! Yeah man – yeah! Load my ass man – load my ass!!!!!!"

"Oh Bob, tell me about him poking your tight little cherry asshole. Oh man that is making me go crazy! Tell me man, tell me!"

"I was fucking scared crazy he was going to slam it in me all the way. Thank goodness he didn't! He put the head right at my hole and then he told me he was going to show me how to go up in a guy's ass without making him scream crazy in pain. He started pushing real slow and let the head of his dick start pushing my hole open. He was real careful to go real slow. After he started, and started getting it open some, then I got real anxious and kept telling him to 'go in me, go in me!' He kept telling me to calm down, he would, but he wanted to go in good and slow, till I got all opened up. He said he wanted all of it in there for a moment before he started ramming on it! Oh man, did he know what in the hell he was doing! Jack, he put that whole fucking rod of his up in my ass and it never hurt at all! Oh, but once he got it up in there and he knew I was open, he turned into some fucking screaming bull! My God man, I'm honest, I don't think some wild fucking two ton bull could have fucked me any harder and rougher than he did that day! Oh my ass was sore! I couldn't hardly walk after he got done. He told me he wanted to be sure I remembered that fuck and that day, for the rest of my life. And I have, and I will – oh my God Jack! – you shooting again? Oh man, you're cummin again? Oh God man, I can't believe that! Man oh man! Once you get in a guy's ass, you really do it don't you? Cum man, cum man – yeah – cum in me!"

"Oh Bob, oh, I'm exhausted! I'm exhausted man!" Jack attempted to say as he once again fell full length across Bob. "Oh man, I've never, never ever thought about anybody ever having sex like you and Brad had that day! Oh God Bob!! What a fucking time you had with him that day! Oh man, I've never been fucked before, but shit man, after hearing about you getting it from that Brad guy, I wish he was here now! Oh man, I'd love to be getting fucked by him!"

"Oh, so my dick is not good enough for you? Is that what you are saying?"

"Oh no Bob, that's not what I mean. No, no! Oh Bob, I was having this crazy thinking about me fucking you while that Brad was fucking me! Oh God man, me on you and him on me! Oh man, I'm getting way to hot over that idea. Bob, you ever played with two guys like that? Oh man, you ever done that?"

"Yes I have, and yes I will every chance I get! And when you get a chance, make sure you are the middle guy! What a feeling to be fucking some good tight ass, and at the same time, having your own ass fucked! Man, oh man, that is living!"

"Bob, I never thought, in my wildest dreams, I'd ever be asking this, but Bob, will you fuck my ass? Please? Please, I need it! This is way too wild for me! Man, I never thought I'd ever be doing anything like this, and now I feel like I want to do everything. That talk about fucking some guy's ass while someone is fucking your own, is way more than I ever thought about wanting, but Bob, is there anyway we can do that with someone?"

The Reunion
Chapter Four:
One Step at a Time

"Oh Bob, what a thought! Oh shit man, that is so hot! I've got to do that! God – for a guy that's never done any of this before, I sure am wanting to do it all now, ain't I?"

"Yeah, you sure are, but I think maybe we had better take it one step at a time. You haven't even been butt fucked yet, and you're wanting to be the middle man in a three-way! I think we need to get you butt fucked first before we move on to more guys. Come on man, lie down here and let me at that ass!"

With those instructions, Jack followed the orders. He immediately pulled out of Bob's back end chambers, and laid down on the bed with his own butt up in the air.

"Hey man, you will go slow getting into me, won't you?" Jack pleaded.

"Yeah, I will, I will! I want you to enjoy this. This will be kind of like my first time with Brad. Slow and easy and letting you have a good time. Only thing is, my dick just ain't as big as Brad's and I'll tell you I wish it was!"

"Thank goodness it's not, from what you told me! His sounds like it just might be a little too big for me to take, or even think about trying to take."

Bob stepped into the bathroom for just a second, and as he came out, he told Jack, "Hey, I'm going to use some of this hand cream they have in the bathroom in your ass so that I can make sure everything slides in nice and neat.

I'm going to finger fuck you some, before I dick fuck you, so I can start getting that old coal mine opened up a little. Now, unless you're used to sticking some hand cream up in your butt, this is probably going to feel kind of weird at first, but just lie there and relax. It's just going to be my fingers at first. You OK?"

"Yeah, I'm OK, just kind of nervous! Just don't slam my ass like you said you did to that Brad, when you first fucked him. I'll need it good and slow!"

"Hey don't worry! I've learned a lot about fucking since that day! That day, I was real ignorant and didn't know what happens if you don't open a guy's ass first! Hey, how's my finger feeling?"

"Oh shit man, it feels great! I've stuck my own finger up in my ass before, but it sure never felt like your finger does. I guess just the being somebody else's finger makes the difference. Bob, that feels fucking good, it really does!"

For some period of time, Bob continued to finger fuck Jack, getting his ass opened up pretty good, so that when he poked his stiff dick up in there, it would all feel good to Jack, and not hurt any.

After having four fingers up into Jack's asshole and performing quite a line up of finger movements and broadening exercises, Bob finally said, "O.K. man! You are ready? I'm going to get in position and then let my dick find its warm and cozy home! You ready to get it in the ass – finally? You ready to get fucked?"

"Yeah, yeah, I'm ready! I'm nervous, I admit, but yeah, I'm ready. Just go slow and easy, OK?"

"Yeah I will! Slow and easy!"

And Bob did. He pointed his dick crown right at the opening, smeared just a little hand cream on it, and started in! Slowly, and going in only a little bit at a time, but succeeding in making a little headway with each push, inch by inch, he was making headway of inching into Jack's virgin, tight, ass.

"Hey man, how you doing? You are now fully fucked man! You now have all of me up in you! How you like having a guy's dick up in you? Does it feel like you got a big Brazilian banana stuck up in there?"

"Oh God Bob, you have your whole dick up in me? Honestly, you have all of it up in there? You've got the whole damn thing up in me?"

"Yeah! I've got the whole thing up in you. You've got my whole rod up in there! How you feeling?"

"Oh Bob, I feel great! I can't imagine feeling this good with your whole dick stuck up in me! Really man, I can't imagine you've stuck all of it up in me and it never hurt any! Oh Bob, if this is getting fucked, fuck me crazy man, fuck me hard! Oh man, now I know why you wanted me to fuck the hell out of you! God, I thought you were crazy, but shit man, now I understand! Oh Bob, fuck me! Let me know I've been fucked! Fuck me man, fuck me!"

That was all the encouragement and words that Bob needed to hear! He knew that he had successfully entered Jacks insides, and now he was told to fuck him good and to fuck him hard! Jack expressed a constant moaning and groaning of, "Yeah man, yeah! Yeah do me! Yeah fuck my ass! Fuck me really hard! Yeah – fuck me!"

As Bob grabbed Jack around the chest and hung on tightly, he pounded his ass like he was making up for all lost time. "I'm fucking the hell out of you man, fucking like shit! You taking it like a man? You liking this fucking man? You liking this?"

Jack managed in a strangled manner to get an answer out that was sort of, "Yeah, yeah! Yeah – fuck me hard, harder! I love it man! I love getting my ass beat up like that! Yeah Bob, fuck my ass raw!"

Just as Jack was asking to get his ass fucked raw, Bob started getting real close to cummin! "Oh Jack! Oh! Oh man – you are about to get some warm assed cum up in you! Oh man, I'm about ready to let it fly! Oh hang on man – you're getting a load of my cream! Oh Jack – your ass is getting it man, it's getting it! Oh man, your ass just got it man! Oh shit man did it fly! Oh shit – I'm fucking exhausted! Oh man – how's your ass feeling? Feeling good? Your insides feeling good and hot, man?"

"Oh man! Oh man! Oh Bob, I never dreamt that getting cum shot up in your ass could feel like that! Oh shit man! Oh, I like that! What a feeling! Oh, it's so warm! Oh, my insides are singing man – they are singing!! Wow, my whole insides feel like it's all coated with cum! Shit man, does it always feel that good to have a guy shoot his milk up in you like that? Oh, wow! Shit – what a feeling! I don't think it feels like that to some gal when she takes a load. I've never had any women ever make good comments about cum feeling like that to her! Wow man, what a feeling! Oh shit man, am I going to have your baby now? God man, if I am, I feel like that kid should be half grown from the way he hit the insides of me. Oh man, what a load! God Bob, how long's it been since you shot off?"

"Hey – a day! Got my rocks off Thursday night right after I got to town. I did some cute little blond guy that I met in the hotel lobby! He didn't have a room reservation for that night, so I made sure he had some place to sleep – so to say! He paid his way with his ass! Fact is, I think maybe he kind of over paid! But then who's counting?"

"Oh God, you mean you brought some guy up here to your room, that you had just met in the lobby? Is that what you mean?"

"Yeah! Hey, you need to help out whenever a guy can, right? Course, got to admit that if he had not been about the cutest thing on this side of town, then maybe he wouldn't have been offered the help, but like I said, cute as hell, and an ass that was as tight as a vice grip!"

"Oh Bob, I can't believe it! You just picked up some guy you didn't know, and you brought him up to your room and fucked his ass? Is that right?"

"Yeah, yeah! Why not? Nothing different than some guy that finds some chick and takes her home for the night. Hey, I thought he was cute, he liked me, and he told me that if I'd let him stay with me for the night, he'd put out for me. That's how I found out he puts out for guys. When he told me that, he didn't even know yet I was into guys! He just took his chances. Paid off though!"

"How old was this guy?"

"Oh probably about twenty-two or twenty-three. Legal, but still on the younger side. Younger, and tighter side, so to say. With all the reunions and other stuff going on in town right now, he couldn't find a room. I found out he was having some problems, so I helped him out. He had missed an earlier plane and so his connection here was all screwed up, and he had to layover till morning, to catch another flight. So I flew him – so to say, while he was here! Laid on his butt, damn near the whole night! So anyway, the load you just took up your ole shit chute was all fresh stuff. No left over stuff! All fresh cummins! Hell, I think I made all of that stuff just while you were fucking my ass. God, for a first timer, you sure did catch on how to fuck an ass fast! How'd you like fucking my ass? Like fucking a guy's ass? Better than a woman's pussy, right?"

"Oh shit man, I guess! I never got that fucking excited when I and Marilyn or any of my old girlfriends did some fucking. Man, a solid firm ass is great! God man, it feels great, just slamming up against a good solid firm muscled ass. And like I said earlier, even before we got ourselves drunk and started doing the fucking stuff, you've got a good looking ass now, and I can be one person that says it fucks good too! Bob, ever get fucked by any of the other high school gang? Any of them know why you and Janet got divorced?"

"Oh, just Shawn Brownly."

"Shawn Brownly!" Jack exclaimed rather wildly. "Shawn Brownly, the quarterback!? You're kidding man, you've got to be kidding! How in the hell did you and Shawn ever do anything together? Bob, the same Shawn Brownly that I'm thinking of?"

"Yip, that one! The dream guy of every high school girl's dreams. Buff, strong, hunky, muscular, toned, handsome, hung like a horse and gay as a basket of posies! We happened to be in a restaurant restroom together about three, four, years ago, and he did not realize who I was. I spoke to him, said 'Hi,' but didn't call him by name, and I guess when I spoke, he kind of took that as a come on, and so anyway after he took a piss, he turned toward me and made some comments about how being by yourself on a Friday night can be really lonesome, and then kind of jerked at his dick. Hey man – that was a definite, 'take it, suck it and use it' signal to me. I figured out pretty quickly he did not realize I already knew who he was, and decided to play the game and not tell him. Well, until later, much later! I wanted to use that body, and I was afraid that if I told him who I was, he'd change his mind."

"So what in the hell happened? You guys do it there in the restroom?"

"Oh no! No, I don't do stuff in a restroom. I asked him if he had someplace we could go to, and he said, 'Yeah, got an apartment real close we can use.' So I said, 'OK, what's the address,' and then we agreed to meet there in half an hour. He never asked me my name till I got to the apartment and then I just told him, 'Butch.' He never asked for a last name. He just said he was Shawn. He still did not realize who I was. But hey, in high school he was the all athletic jock and I was a nobody, so why should I expect him to know me anyway! Right?"

"Yeah – guess so. Hate to admit it, but yeah, that's the way stuff goes most of the time. So you called yourself Butch, instead of Bob? What, just to keep him off guard?"

"Yeah, I didn't want him to realize who I was. I wanted to keep that a secret for awhile yet. So, anyway, when I got to the apartment, it was really bare. Hardly any furniture. I made a comment about it being kind of empty, and he told me that yeah, it was, but this was just his hideout place for his playing around. Then he looked at me, laughed and said, 'My wife don't know about it.' Man, I could not believe it! There I was, in Shawn Brownly's private, 'gay playroom apartment,' about to fuck around with him, and now finding out that he was fucking guys without his wife knowing it, and – that he had an extra secret apartment, just for it! Fuck man, talk about one exciting fucking session. Me and the ole high school quarterback!"

"Bob this is too much! That guy was always supposed to be the top of everything. He could do no wrong while he was in school, and then he's married, and keeps a secret apartment to play with guys in! Wow! God the nerve of some guys! Do you guys still do stuff together or whatever happened? Did he find out who you were?"

"Yeah he found out after one hot and heavy sex session we had that night. When he told me that was a secret apartment, and obviously not his home, I asked him how long he could play before he needed to head home. He told me his wife was out of town till the next afternoon, so he could play as long as we wanted. I told him, 'Great,' and for the next six hours we did every type of gay sex act that either one of us could think to do. Now don't freak out over this Jack, but I even gave him about three quarters of a fisting that night too."

"Fisting, what do you mean, fisting? You mean, putting your fist up in his ass? Is that what you mean?"

"Yeah, yeah, that's fisting! It's kind of like the ultimate of getting fucked in the ass! Some great feelings with something really big stuck up in your ass. Lot of guys are really into it! It's real popular with the leather guys. Jack, that's why I have that gay, leather man's, sticker on my car. That's kind of my signal to guys that know what it means. I mean, not all leather guys do fisting, but a lot do. And my attitude is, ask, I just might say 'Yes.' "

"So what you mean is, you kind of gave him three quarters of a fisting? Is that what you mean?"

"I couldn't get his asshole opened up far enough to take my whole hand, so I didn't get it all the way in. Well, not that night anyway."

"Not that night!? Meaning – you did him later? You guys did it again?"

"Oh yes, oh yes! That first night, he was fucking my ass for probably the third or fourth time that night, and while he was in the process of dumping my ass full of some quarterback's cum shot, I just kind of laid there and then said, 'Man, when we were in school together I never imagined that some day I'd have your dick stuck up in my ass and getting all of your cum shot up in me!' "

"Oh my God Bob, what in the hell did he do?"

"Well, at first he almost screamed, 'What?' Got to remember he was in the process of shooting off in my ass right when he heard that, and he had some real problems trying to manage his dick and his brain at the same time. He finally rammed me one more good ram, and I mean one like maybe it was going to be the last one, and he pulled out and flipped me over and asked who in the hell I was. I laid there and just told him I was one of his high school classmates, but I knew he didn't know that, and since I didn't want him to change his mind about getting together, I decided to keep it a secret, and then

I added, 'Like, you keep this apartment a secret.' "

"Was he pissed? What'd he do?"

"You know, I think at first he was kind of pissed. Well, maybe a little afraid that his secret would get out, but then after I convinced him that his secret was definitely safe with me, since I wanted us to get together some more, and maybe get all of my fist up in his ass, he kind of started, liking the idea of maybe having a steady playmate that he could call on and trust. He kept asking me who I was, and even though I told him my name about three times, he just finally said, 'Oh, wait – you're that guy that had that good looking girl friend all through school, right? Janet – her name was Janet – right?'

"I told him, right that was me. Then he told me, 'God man, you don't look the same! You were real skinny! You the same guy?' I told him, yeah, I was the same one. Then, and much to my surprise he added, 'Shit man, if you had looked like this, back then, I'd been fucking your ass a long time ago!' Shocked the shit out of me! After that, I found out he had been playing around with some of the other county football players, whenever he got a chance. Hell man, the whole fucking time he was the high school football quarterback and the main man on campus, he was out messing around with other football players from the other teams. God, I wonder what in the hell it was like for those guys out on the field when they were playing each other! Talk about tackling some guy. Tackle him, then while you're on top of him, whisper in his ear about how good his ass was the last time they met out in the old barn!"

"Oh shit man, imagine the guys that fuck each other, then playing against each other out on a football field. Damn man, the juices must have been flowing during those games! So what else did you guys talk about, what else happened?"

"He asked about Janet and wondered what ever happened. I think when I told him we were divorced, and my being gay was the reason was what kind of calmed him down and he knew maybe things could really work out for us to get together once in awhile. He told me he got married about three years out of high school, simply because everybody, family included, expected it and kept asking him when was he going to get married. He said that he finally found himself a girl and got married just to shut 'em up! He told me she had no idea, well as far as he knew anyway, about his playing with guys. He said their marriage was pretty calm and tame. He still felt like it was still a stage play for his family and everybody else. He finally admitted that he really was glad that he finally had someone from his prior years that knew the real him, and somebody that he could have a good friendship with! We played with each other, and I finally got him fully fisted, before I moved. I was really hoping to see him while I was back, but I keep getting his voice mail and haven't heard back from him yet."

"Oh so he's the reason you're staying at the hotel instead of at your Mom and Dad's place, uh?"

"Well, maybe part of it! But Diane's fifteenth year reunion is this week-end also, so since she and Dwayne and the kids are at the house, I told Mom and Dad that I'd just stay at the hotel where the reunion was and make things that much easier at the house. Beside, ever since I came out and let the family know I'm gay, Dwayne looks at me kind of funny, and I'm not sure yet if it's because he can't stand me for being gay, or if he's hoping we can fuck each other. I just decided that staying away from him as much as possible was probably a good thing!"

"Yeah Bob, it probably is! Would you fuck him if he indicated he wanted to do it? What would you do?"

"I'd fuck the hell out of him! He's a hot man, he's hot! Yeah, I know he's my brother-in-law, but shit man, I'm sure that if he was gutsy enough to tell me he wanted to do it, he sure as hell is not going to tell anybody we did it! So if he ever told me he wanted to, hell yes I'd fuck that ass of his!"

"Well, what if he wanted to fuck you? Then what?"

"Then I'd be in fucking heaven! I've seen that dick of his when we were kids and went skinny dipping, long time ago, and it is a fucking monster! I'd love to feel that up inside of me! Ever since they got married, I've always wondered just what it felt like for Diane to get poked with that thing! Hey – I guess it must feel pretty good, they've got four kids from her getting poked with it!"

"So you think maybe Shawn might try to get in touch with you while you're in town?"

"Well, I was hoping he would, but now since this has happened tonight, I really don't care if he does or not! If he calls, and finally tells me he wants to do it, then we'll fuck if he can, but if not, I'm getting some good stuff anyway, so I don't care. But hey Jack – I've kind of been wondering – why are you staying at the hotel instead of at your Mom and Dad's place? Were you hoping for some extra fun too?"

"No, that's not the reason. Course, not objecting to what is happening, but Mom and Dad are in Hawaii. The whole idea that I was going to be coming home for five days, just was not enough for them to, maybe, consider changing their Hawaii days, to maybe, just next week? Hell man, I've known, and they've known for six months that I'd be coming home this week, but let's not interfere with travel plans that – had not even been made yet! They told me to just stay at the house, but I decided staying here and not even going to the house would be better. I figured that if anything is wrong at the house, when they get back, then I can't be accused of it. My sister Julie takes her kids over there and lets them get into everything and never tells them to keep their hands off of anything, so I just decided to stay away. Beside, now I am damn glad I did! Damn glad! This is good! I've obviously been needing something new in my life, and I think I just found it! You tired? You look like you're about to fall asleep."

"Yeah man, yeah I am. Let's get some sleep so I can go back and get my car in the morning. What time is it anyway? Oh shit man! Hell it's about time for the sun to start coming up! God – we have played for what, three, four hours? Yeah, we need to get some sleep. Come here, let me hug you while we go to sleep, OK? Can I do that?"

"Yes you can man, you sure can! That is going to feel good. It's been a long time since I've had someone hug me while I fall asleep. You can hug me tight if you want!"

The Reunion
Chapter Five:
That Tasted Good!

After what turned out to be only a few hours of sleep, both men woke up and had morning boners.

"I've got to go take a piss man! I'm about ready to wet myself if I don't go pee right away!" Jack said as he jumped out of bed.

"What, wait!" Bob yelled as he jumped out of bed too. "Hey man, head for the shower! I want to stand in front of you while you piss! I want you to pee on me. I wanna feel that warm water hitting my skin and running down off of my body!"

"Bob? You sure? You want me to pee on you? You sure?"

"Yeah, I'm sure man – I'm sure! Jack you are going to find out there are a hell of a lot of new things to experience that you just have never done before. Yeah, I want you to pee on me, and if you decide you want to see what it's like, then I'll pee on you! Really man, things can be fun! Things that everybody always said you can't do. Hell, maybe that's the reason they are so much fun. You've always been told, no, no – can't do that, don't do that!"

Jack stepped into the shower and Bob quickly followed.

"Hey man, come on, pee on me! Yeah – yeah, I like that! I know Jack, this is weird isn't it? The first time I had a guy tell me to pee on him, I about crapped, but if you like to do some different and fun stuff once in awhile, letting somebody stand there and pee on you is fun."

As Jack let his stream flow, Bob stooped down in front of Jack so that he could let the pee hit him right under the chin. Jack rather nervously aimed his dick at Bob's chest and kinda uttered an, "Ok, if this is what you want. Shit man, I never thought I'd ever be peeing on the front of some guy. This is different man, really different. Whatever happened the first time you peed on some guy? How did that happen?"

"It was a camping weekend once. Me and about five other guys were out camping and fishing up beside Ole Man Lake, and it was probably about three o'clock in the morning, and I had to get up and go take a piss. You know all of the campsites up there are really off by themselves, so if you gotta go take a pee, you just go outside of your tent and pee. You don't go to a porta potty or a restroom building. Well, anyway I went outside, walked just a little away from the campsite, pulled it out of my briefs and started taking a piss. That's what I was doing when all of a sudden I heard some guy say, 'Oh man, I like the looks of that! Hey guy, pee on me, please. I wanna feel that hitting me. Come on man, pee on me, please!' "

Standing there letting it continue to flow down and onto Bob's chest and gut, he anxiously asked, "He just showed up? Was he one of your group?"

"No, no he wasn't. I didn't know him. He just showed up from one of the other campsites. He moved over in front of my pee stream, sank down on his knees, reached out and took ahold of my dick and aimed it at his chin, and let my piss soak it all wet. I finally got all drained, and he leaned forward, licked the end of my dick kinda dry, then stood up, looked at me and said, 'Thanks man, thanks! That tasted good!' Then he just turned and walked away. He walked back over toward another campsite that honestly I did not see until after he got there. It was not in plain view from our site."

"Well – was he naked or did he have clothes on?"

"No, he had some cute little tight shorts on. They were all wet when he went back to his campsite, but yeah, he had shorts on."

"My God Bob – did you ever see that guy again while you were out there camping?"

"Oh yeah, yeah, sure did! The next morning about, oh, maybe six or six thirty, he went driving by in his Park Ranger Jeep. He was one of the Park Rangers there! He drove by, looked over, saw me, and just casually waved."

"Did the other guys in your group see him, or know what had happened the night before?"

"Well, after they saw him wave at me, they did. Billy, one of our group saw him wave, saw me wave back, and then asked if I knew that guy or not. I kinda grinned and said, 'Well, kinda.' Of course, he then asked, 'Kinda? What do you mean, kinda?'"

"I grinned real big again, and told him, 'Well, I can say I know him well enough that he's gotta wash my pee out of his shorts.'"

"Billy looked at me really confused, which I expected and asked, 'Wash your pee out of his shorts!? What in the hell are you saying?'"

"So then I told him what had happened during the night. He stood there and just stared at me. He kept saying stuff like, 'What? What? Where did this happen? When did this happen? Did you know he was a park Ranger?'"

"I told him that, 'Nope, I did not know that he was a Ranger, until right then, watching him drive by in the Ranger Jeep. After all, when he was getting pissed on, he did not have a uniform on.'"

"Oh God Bob, was this group of guys, that you were camping with, gay guys or straight guys?"

"Oh, they were gay. This was like about maybe five years ago. That was during my time of kinda switching life styles. Yeah, they were all gay guys, so they all got a kick out of what happen when I was just out taking a piss."

"Did you ever see that Ranger again? How long did you guys camp there?"

"Well, that little pee session happened on Friday night – well actually early Saturday morning, and we didn't break camp, until about sunset Monday night, cause that was Labor Day, so we had a long weekend. So we were there for three more days after the early morning pissing session."

Now having fully drained his plumbing while learning about Bob's first, 'pee on me,' session, he told Bob, "I'm done man, I'm done. I kinda think that you telling me about the Ranger guy getting you to pee on him, did make me pee longer than usual, but now, it's all done. What're we gonna do now?"

"Hey my friend! That is up to you? You can go jump in bed and give me a minute or two to rinse some hot man pee off of me, or you could wait here while I take a piss. And while I'm in the process of letting my bladder drain dry, you can decide if you wanna play the part, that the Park Ranger did that night, and feel some nice warm pee slide down off of your shoulders and down around that big bush of hair you got showing down there, around that dick of death, that you've got sticking out there. Which my man, which?"

"I'm not going to bed without you! I'm staying here, but I'm not sure, just yet, if I can let you spray me like I did you. I'm gonna stand up and watch you start peeing, and then I want you to just spray my legs and see if I can get up enough nerve to stoop down and let you spray my chest. O.K.? Is that O.K.?"

"That's more than O.K. with me. Sounds good to me, and besides, I gotta pee. I'm gonna spray your legs, and if you decide to stoop down, great, but if not, no big deal! Hang tight man, you are gonna get peed on for the first time man. Well, I guess the first time, right?"

"Oh shit yes man, hell yes. Hey, Bob, tell me some more about that camping trip you guys were on and see if me hearing some of that gets me all excited to where I can decide to grab you dick and aim it up at my chest, and let you spray me up higher."

"Oh O.K. Can do! Well, like I was saying, Billy got a real kick out of it, and then he hollered for the other guys to come over, and he told them what happened. Of course the whole group got a real kick out of it. He told them about the guy just driving by in the Ranger Jeep, and how he waved. Everybody wanted to know what this guy looked like, how was he built and anything else that I could tell them. I told 'em that he looked like he was probably twenty four or twenty five, I thought he stood about five feet eleven or six foot tall, big broad shoulders, real trim waist, and of course I never got to see his dick, since he had shorts on. But, he was hot – real hot. So anyway, then the group decided that we needed to see if he was into more than just getting peed on, and to see if we could maybe gang bang him if possible."

"Oh God man, oh shit! Yeah man, yeah, this is making me hot as hell man, I've gotta let you spray me as much as you can."

And with that strong statement, Jack did grab Bob's dick, aimed the piss up and on his chest and just below his chin line. Then, he anxiously asked, as he watched the warm yellow piss hit his chest and then flow down his torso, toward his feet, "So what did you guys do? Did you ever get to gang bang the guy? Did you guys play with him?"

"Oh yes, oh yes! He was quite the little gay whore. Well, maybe I should not call him a whore since he did not charge, but he sure was easily available once we let him know we all wanted him and thought he was hot."

"Oh God man, oh shit, this is stuff I've never heard any guy talk about, and it is turning me on like crazy. Jack, how did you guys get him to let you play with him, or whatever happened?"

"Well, it was kinda up to me, since I was the only one that had talked to the guy, and so we decided to keep an eye on his site, and whenever he showed up again, I was to go over and tell him thanks for what had happened. Then I was to tell him that, 'I had never done that before, and I did find it rather exciting, and some of the other guys in our group had wondered if he'd be interested in doing that for them.' A big smile came across his face and I thought for a minute he was going to start jumping up and down. He told me to go tell the guys – at least the ones that wanted to play – that if they wanted to shower on him, drink a lot of beer, warm if possible, and fight off peeing until he could get there about ten o'clock. He said he had to stay on duty until about nine thirty, and just as fast as he could, he'd be over to our campsite and ready to get hit with some good warm piss, and spray anyone that wanted to get sprayed. We found out later that he was the Ranger that had checked us in on Friday morning, although none of us paid any attention to him at that time. He was the one that had assigned us our campsite, cause when he saw all of us coming in together, with no women, and using one campsite, he had high hopes that maybe he could get something going with us. That's why he was out there watching our campsite that first night. Everything worked out just like he had hoped it would. He said he just knew that one of us would have to get up in the middle of the night and go take a piss. And, of course, that 'one' happened to be me. He told us that since our campsite is much more remote than all of the others, that's the reason he uses the campsite next to ours. Out there on that little peninsula of land, it's just the two campsites. He likes is out there, and he watches for the right people to assign the other campsite to. He told us that when he saw all of us together, with no wives, he just knew we were the 'right' ones. Before the weekend was over, he told us that he wanted to be gang banged by all of us, just as fast as we could do him. He wanted to get fucked by one of us, and have all of the rest of us standing by in a line, so that just as soon as one guy pulls out, he wants the next one to go in, and then take all of us just as fast as he can. Late Sunday night we did, and then he begged us to do it all over again. That man loves to be fucked hard and fast and by as many guys as he can get together at the same time."

Just as Bob was saying, 'and, of course, that 'one' happened to be me,' he ran out of fluid flowing from his dick, and at the same time watched Jack move his hand around on his chest and his stomach, sliding the warm piss around and letting it soak into his skin, as if he was using it as a skin lotion.

"So, I guess you must have liked that right? You're rubbing it in like it's something that is supposed to be there."

"Oh yeah man, oh yeah! You know Bob, right now I'd like for my parents to be standing here and watching what I'm doing. Hell man, I'd like for Marilyn to be watching this too. Show her what some good sex fun can be all about. As for Mom and Dad, I've decided that it is finally time for me to grow up and quit doing just what they want. Hey man – if they find out sometime of what I've been learning and doing since last night, I'm sure both of them would have a major heart attack just trying to tell their holy minister of how sinful I've been. I've always had to listen to them and do just as they say, and man, things are gonna change now."

"Yeah, I agree. Things need to change. And right now the change is us getting rinsed off, getting dry, and getting back in bed so we can follow through with what we started, before we both needed to come take a piss."

"Yes, and I still want you to tell me what your camping group did with that Park Ranger, and how that all worked out, O.K.?"

Both men did rinse off – also took some pleasures of helping his respective partner, lift up, and help get fully rinsed some of his hanging parts, so that everything was fully and completely rinsed.

As the men finished getting each other dry, then hanging the towels back onto the rack, they headed for the bed, and as Bob rolled Jack over onto his stomach, he said, "And this is what all six of us did to that Park Ranger." And with that statement made, he mounted Jack's back, pointed his rod at Jack's anus, and then said, "We fucked him crazy. Saturday night – Sunday night – and then again early Monday morning. That was one Park Ranger that got what he was wanting, in one hell of a big way! When everything was done, he had had his ass fucked over and over, and he in turn had fucked the hell out of each of us, and then he told us, 'Thanks men thanks! The park's closing down for the winter, after this week, and I have finally gotten what I have been praying for all summer. Every weekend I kept watching for the right car load of guys to come in, and until I saw you guys coming in, and found out that you were all together, I thought my whole summer was going right down the drain without me getting what I'd been watching for all summer. Then he gave us each his phone number and told us to call him before we headed up to the park anytime next summer, and we would not have to pay an entrance, nor a camping fee. Then he laughingly admitted that by doing that, that way, he'd know just when one of us was gonna be there, and he'd also know what campsite to reserve for us. And yes, the next year, I and a couple of the other guys did take advantage of the free passes, and his hot tight little ass, a number of times."

"The next year – did you guys just fuck him or did you guys do the pissing thing again?"

"Oh yeah, we did the pissing thing again – and again – and again. Hey, one time he saw Tommy starting to take a piss, and Johnny, the Ranger, ran up to him, and made him stop peeing long enough to push Tommy's dick up in his ass, and then had him finish peeing, in his ass. The first time when we did any peeing with him, was a learning session for us, and so all winter long, the whole group of us, whenever we were together with one of the other guys, we – so to say – we practiced. So yeah, ole Park Ranger Johnny got a lot of experience the next summer, fucking, getting fucked, peeing on someone and getting peed on himself, plus all of the sucking – the giving and the getting. Well, that kinda happened to all of us, I guess!"

All of a sudden the conversation about Johnny and the park situation became a very moot point, and the entire conversation and attention was directed, completely and fully, at Jack getting Bob's hunk of meat up, and into his ass, and then letting it all come flying, after only a couple of minutes.

"Oh shit Bob, damn! Wow! What in the hell can I say. I kinda have to admit that years and years of experience sure does pay off, don't it? And I don't particularly mean for you, I mean for the guy under you getting the hell fucked out of him. You sure as hell know how to do it, and I guess now all I can do is hope, like hell, that you will be my instructor, and teach me everything that you can, so that I will be able to take some guy's ass and make him feel just as good as I do right now."

The Reunion
Chapter Six:
Plus Another Five Years

Walking into the old downtown bar, that he and Jack had visited five years earlier, Bob firmly stated, "Come on guys, the first round is on me! We've got things to celebrate here tonight!"

As Bob, Jack, Sam, Troy, Phillip and Shawn walked into the bar, Bob looked over to the bartender and said, "Hey, we're here."

The bartender then responded, "Oh, hi guys! I've got your table ready over here. Thanks for the call. Makes things easier when we know ahead of time when a group is coming in."

As they approached the table, Bob then asked the bartender, "Hey, you used to have an older man in here as a bartender when we were in high school, during those day when we were too young to get beer, and he was still here five years ago when we were in town for our reunion. Is he still here? You know which man I'm referring to?"

Without a smile on his face, the bartender answered, "Oh yeah, I know who you are talking about. That was old George. One day suddenly, about three years ago, he was behind the bar, and just suddenly collapsed. He had been a bartender here for more than thirty years, and as I know you found out when you attempted to find our old name in the phone book, the bar has been re-named, 'Old Georgie's,' and he is the old George being referred to. He was a great guy. Thanks for asking about him. I'm sure he is listening to us, now, from wherever he is. Thanks."

Then rather solemnly replying, Jack replied, "God I'm sorry to hear that! Bob and I were in here five years ago when we were in town, and that man really took good care of us. He finally had to tell us that it was time to close, and he insisted that he call us a cab, since he knew both of us were way beyond the driving stage. I'm sorry to hear that, but I am glad to hear about the name change. He sure was a great guy five years ago, and fifteen and sixteen years ago, also, when Bob and I tried to act old enough to buy beer in here, and he was just too sharp to let us do it."

"Yeah, we miss him a lot. But I do assume that since you've now come in, you have also noticed that the décor and the attitude of the bar has changed too. Right?"

Laughing some, and with a big grin on his face, Bob replied, "Well, yes! Especially with the bare ass showing on that guy in the picture on the beach, and maybe that enormous crotch in that other picture. Gone gay? Right?"

"Yeah – hope it's O.K. with all of you guys?"

Again with a big grin on his face, Bob replied, "O.K. – oh yeah! We're all gay guys, but since we're all now from out of town – but three of us did go to high school here – we did not know of the change – but to be honest, glad for it. Now I think we'll be a little bit more comfortable having our little 'catch-up session,' than we would have been, without the changes. Thanks man."

Following the little up-date on the bar, the bartender then asked, "O.K. guys – moving on – what are you guys drinking?"

The bartender took the drink orders, told the men he'd be right back with them, and as he left, Bob stated, "Damn, sorry to hear about that." Then looking at Troy, Sam, Shawn and Phillip, he added, "That man was part of one wild and exciting night for us, wasn't he Jack?"

With everybody now looking at Jack, almost all of the additional men asked, "What? Why? What happened?"

"Well, it was kinda a lot like tonight, guys. Class reunion, two guys that really did not wish to be around all of the rest that are now trying to express and convince everybody of how successful they are in life, how happy their marriages are, how all of their children are on the dean's list, and all of the other crap that is still going on back there, at the hotel, and that banquet room full of wannabes. We wanted to just get out of there, and of course as you all know, that is the night Bob and I found out about each other in a real way. We ended up here for probably four or five hours, then over to the hotel."

Jack listened to Bob, then added, "We were both going through some crappy times, and that night helped both of us kinda get our heads on right. And thankfully, since it was only about a month later – and me being in a much better mood – I found Sam, and with his help, we finally got my life straightened out, and here we are today. And seriously men, if it had not been for all of the talking and some of the other stuff that happened that night, I know damn well, I would never have been doing the right stuff to be able to meet a guy like Sam." Then leaning slightly sideways, he planted a large kiss on his partners lips. Then firmly stated, as he looked at Sam, "Love you man, love you."

Thanking the bartender for the drinks that he had just delivered to the table, Bob then told the group, "Well, that night and that conversation was good for me as well as for Jack. I thought I had my life pretty well on track, but after some of the conversations with Jack, and some of the instructions that I was much better at, in 'giving' – instead of 'actually doing it' – made me leave that reunion with a lot more self respect, and when you have more self-respect, and you feel good about yourself, people like Troy – here – shows up." Then looking at Troy and giving him a big smooch on the face, Bob added, "Fifth of next month – our fourth year anniversary! He's my man! Love him!" And with that statement made, in unison and without instruction, all of the table-full, raised their glasses and stated, "Congratulations, congratulations!" The click of glass could be heard throughout the bar.

With just a slight silence, and everybody wondering who was going to speak next, Shawn then spoke up and said, "I know, I know. All of you are wondering about me and how I happened to be here with my man, and not my woman! Right?"

Almost in union, the men answered, "Yeah, yeah."

Bob was the only one that did not question. He offered an explanation.

"Hey guys. Things change. Times change. Attitudes change. And for some people, their lives change, don't they Shawn?"

Grinning rather openly, Shawn looked at Bob and replied, "Oh yeah, oh yeah! Five years ago, while ole Bob and Jack were here, at a class reunion, wishing things were a little different, Phillip and I were truly making things different. I had finally told ole Sally Ann that I loved guys, and especially one, more than the married life, and within a week, Phillip and I were in Maui having a 'honeymoon.' Divorce to follow up with, but none the less, we were then together. Bob finally got a call from me after we got back and we got all settled, and I explained why he did not hear from me while he was in town. And it is because of that conversation, after we were back from Hawaii, and after his and Jack's time together, that we are here today. Bob and I had shared some secret times and he finally convinced me that secrecy is 'fake living.' He is the one that really got me to understand that who I am – is the real me – and the who I am trying to be – is a fake me. He helped me understand that being a high school kid is one thing, but to be a true man, to myself and to my lover, is being the real true thing. So – chest up – face out – we are here at the class reunion, as a couple. I just know that, that banquet hall has gotten one hell of a lot louder and a lot more active since we all introduced ourselves, and introduced our partners, and then excused ourselves. With all of the chit-chat that is now going on back there – once the three little musketeers, and their husbands had left the room – it's gotta be one hell of a lot more active. How I wish I was a little mouse in the corner, listening to all of them and their questions and comments. The gib-gab has got to be really flowing, now! Now they've really got some new stuff to talk about, rather than how great their jobs are, how great their kids are, their degrees, their vacations, their marriages and everything else that is so great about them. I'm glad we are all together, and in another five years guys, we will all be together again, and maybe – just maybe – have some new members joining us in the group. I saw a couple of guys' faces looking pretty damn jealous – as we stood – for who we really are."

You Want What?
Chapter One:
On the Bus

"I want to suck your cock!"

"What!? You want what!? What did you say!?"

"I want to suck your cock. You are so damn hot, you make me all hot and bothered, and I want to suck on you."

"Holy shit man! What in the hell are you saying? I don't even know you! Who in the hell are you?"

Just as Mike, the potential receiver of this offered gift, of an unrequested and unexpected blow job, was expounding in a very shocked and profound manner the question of, "Who in the hell are you," the city bus pulled to a stop. The bus doors opened and the driver waited as the very shocked and shaken Mike, and his new, but unknown, 'acquaintance' stood at the door of the bus.

In a state of shock and disbelief, Mike looked at the young man, the young man that had just made the very bold, very unexpected, and very shocking statement. Looking at him directly in the face, expressing some degree of a 'state of shock,' Mike then turned and silently stepped up, and into the bus. The young man quietly followed, without any additional words.

With the bus seats all being full, Mike grabbed for a wrist strap and planted his feet firmly to avoid any movement when the bus moved forward. The young man grabbed the strap immediately in front of Mike's. He grabbed the strap, turned to face the front of the bus, and immediately fell backwards, and onto Mike, as the bus lurched forward and pulled away from the curb. He obviously and purposely, had not planted his feet on the floor, quite as solidly as Mike had done. His falling was accomplished with much skill and a great degree of correct aim. He landed just where he had planned.

"Oh, I'm sorry!" The young man immediately expressed to Mike, as if his fall had been a very bad mistake. "Oh sir, I'm sorry! I did not mean to do that!"

Re-positioning himself, Mike managed an, "Oh that's OK. Standing up in these busses, you've really got to be ready when the bus moves."

"Yeah, I guess so! Hope I didn't make you drop anything." The young man expressed, as he turned toward Mike, and looked down as if to see if anything had fallen to the floor.

Now being very suspicious and curious about this young man's profound statement at the bus stop, and his now rather obvious 'faked stumble,' Mike watched closely as the young man turned and looked down. Mike immediately knew that it was not the floor that the young man was now looking at, and that his eyes certainly were not directed to the floor, but only down far enough to have his eye sight stop right at the level of his hidden manhood. Knowing that his crotch was now being rather, 'checked out' by this young man, made Mike somewhat proud, but also slightly embarrassed to think that another man was actually wanting to see his dick.

Pulling his head back up from looking down, the young man then added, "Oh – I guess everything is OK. Looks like everything is OK. Everything looks OK."

Returning to his 'normal' front facing position, the young man immediately took advantage of the action in front of him, with a lady getting up from her seat, stepping into the isle, and he reacting very appropriately by stepping back to give the lady sufficient room to stand. His movement backwards, rather 'unexpectedly' forced his body, and especially his hips to move up to a direct contact position with Mike. Immediately Mike stepped back, but then rather, quite quickly, re-positioned himself directly under his wrist strap. The young man stood stoic. His position, although perhaps just slightly moved to the back was within a normal standing position to where it did not look abnormal. As Mike re-gained his footing and his 'proper position,' the two men were now in a much more full frontal and rather protruding hip 'hugging' position. Mike did not move! For a very slight moment, he almost did, then immediately he decided to just stand his ground. True, they truly were making body contact, but with the passengers up toward the front getting up and rather forcing the standing passengers to move back a little, the contact was not going to be out of the ordinary, nor the normal, but for Mike it certainly was the very unusual. The very, very unusual as he mentally pondered everything that was happening since the moment just before the bus pulled up to the curb, to pick him and this rather 'unusual acting' passenger up.

As Mike gripped the wrist strap with his left hand, and placed his right hand on the back rest of the seat to his right, and slightly forward one row, he noticed that although the street was not really quite 'that rough' the young man standing in front of himself was creating a little more torso action than what was probably necessary. And, all of that action was being transferred directly to, and slightly below his belt line area. Mike knew that in this very public, and thankfully very crowded city bus, he was allowing this young man – a young man that looked like perhaps ten years younger than he was – who's name he did not even know – nor as far as he knew, had he ever talked to before, to rub his ass up against his crotch area, and obviously experience some level of sexual enjoyment, right there on the city bus. As Mike stood there, holding his body firm against the unnecessary actions of being rubbed up against, and in the crotch area no less, Mike told himself, "This guy is gay! He is gay and looking for action! He's actually attempting to play with me right here on the bus. And God, I'm actually letting him do it! He's rubbing my dick with his butt!"

As Mike stood firm in his place, and of course as the young man did the same, the bus pulled over to the curb to load and unload some additional passengers. This created movement within the bus, and as a passenger from the back of the bus squeezed past to get off, everybody that was standing were forced to shift and move. The young man obviously was standing in-wait for this right moment to occur, as he was forced to move slightly to allow the other passenger to squeeze by, his right hand 'just happened' to drop down, slightly to the rear, and then most conveniently, right onto the hidden crotch area that his ass had so very conveniently been sliding up against, only a moment before.

Shocked and rather confusingly, Mike realized that he was now, secretly, being groped by this young man, and right in middle of a city bus, full of people! In his shock, Mike did not react to the grope and the feel, but with it happening so suddenly and so fast, he really did not know how he should have reacted, or would have reacted, if he had known, beforehand, that he was actually going to get a hand in the crotch, and have his dick felt, right in the middle of a public bus. Realizing that it had now actually happened, he pondered at just why he was not furiously mad that this guy – some gay guy – had felt him up – had touched his dick, and had actually done it there in an absolutely public place.

"You get off at 83rd Street, right?" The young man asked as he turned his head slightly toward Mike.

"Uh, uh – yeah, yeah!" Mike managed to utter in complete shock and bewilderment. He was very confused, and bewildered in just how this young man, a young man that he did not know, already knew just which stop he got off at.

"Got time for a quick cup of coffee at Jessie's Cafe before you head for the house?" He asked Mike.

Really not knowing for sure just how that question should be replied to, Mike immediately decided that a quick cup of coffee was definitely necessary if, for no other reason, than to find out just who this guy was, and to make a very strong impression on him that he definitely was not the type of guy that gets his dick sucked off by other guys, and certainly does not have that type of a question asked of him in public.

Mike had decided that, whoever this guy was, he definitely needed to be put in his place and told not to come onto guys, telling them that he wants to suck on their dicks and also grope them in public places, unless he really wanted to be carried away in a city medic van.

"Yeah, yeah I can. You get off there too?"

"Yeah, I live pretty close to 83rd and Miller Street, so I can get off there and walk the rest of the way."

That statement was the last of the verbal interchange, for the following eight or ten minutes that it took for the bus to get to the corner of 83rd Street. Verbal interchange! Just verbal! At each stop, of which there were three before they got to 83rd Street, the young man very successfully managed to re-enact the previous – step aside – move up closer – drop the hand – reach back – do a grope and feel, and then re-position himself for the next short drive. Mike learned quickly that as the bus made each stop, he could expect to feel the groping fingers cup around his crotch, and his dick, and each time the grip got just ever so much more forceful and strong. Not wishing to be the center of any major 'news item' of the day, Mike decided to let it all pass, especially since he was now fully convinced that nobody on the bus could see the actions, nor the groping, and that he would simply straighten this young man out, once they got off of the bus and were in a more private place. He also knew that having this young man standing close to him was now, definitely a good thing since he did realize that due to the, 'hand on the crotch' actions that had been happening, he knew he was starting to get an erection, even though he did not approve of the actions, and did not wish to be fondled by some man. He knew it was some guy touching him, and even knowing that, he had started to get hard. Just the idea of any other person touching him down there was, in his mind, of course going to make any man get hard.

Pulling into the curb line at 83rd Street, the young man politely excused himself as he worked his way to the front of the bus, and Mike immediately followed. They were the only two passengers to exit at 83rd Street.

Being at the bus stop now, and all alone, as the bus pulled away, the young man looked at Mike, smiled widely and then firmly stated, "I want you! Really man, I've been watching you for days now, and I want some of that!"

Quickly looking around to make sure nobody was within ear shot, Mike demanded, "Who in the hell are you? Just who in the hell are you? What in the hell makes you think that I want to have you suck me off? I am not gay! I don't play with guys! I'm married!"

"Come on. Let's walk so nobody wonders why we are just standing here. I figured you were married. But man, you are so damn hot to me that I decided the other day that I just had to see if I had any chance with you at all. I waited until right when the bus was ready to stop at our stop, so that if I really pissed you off real bad, then I didn't think you'd hit me if the bus full of people was there. I've seen you there at the bus stop and on the bus for like two weeks now, and I've watched you get off and walk away from the bus every day. I've made fucking sure I was on that side of the bus so I could watch you and your ass, walk away from the bus. I'm Jamie. My name is Jamie."

"Uh, Jamie, uh I'm Mike. Uh, Jamie – you can't just go up to guys and tell them that you want to suck on them. Jamie, you just can't do that!"

"Yeah I know, but man, if I ever found out that you were a gay guy and not married, and I never told you that I wanted some of you, I'd have been really pissed at me. Man, I decided I just had to get real gutsy and just see what happened. Mike, I've never done this before, but with you, I had to take a chance. Mike, please don't report me to the police or anything, I just wanted to see if I could do it with you. Man, you just turn me on!"

"Jamie, I'm not going to report you to anybody. Nothing happened. Well yeah! You did keep grabbing me and feeling my dick, but I mean, I'm not mad at you. Maybe a little confused, but not mad. Jamie, what is it about me that makes you so excited? I'm just a normal guy."

"No Mike, no! To me you are no normal guy! I like the way you look. You are a real man! You look like you might be about ten or eleven years older than I am, and I like older guys. I've never had any fun with guys my own age. I like guys that are more mature. I like the way you look. I like the way you're built! You're hot man! Hot! You used to be in athletics in school, right? You've got a hot body. I really do want to see it naked. Mike, I've already told you the ultimate of things I can tell you when I told you I wanted to suck on you, so if I tell you that I want to see you naked, I don't think that's much more than what I've already told you, right?"

"Jamie, how old are you?"

"I'm twenty four. How old are you Mike?"

"You were pretty good guessing. I'm thirty six. And yeah, I used to be what they called somewhat of a wrestling star, when I was in high school. Not good enough to get college scholarships, but did O.K. in high school."

"Oh shit man! Oh shit. Mike do you wrestle anymore? Oh man! I'd love to be wrestling with you! Oh man! Oh just the idea of getting to grab hold of you and kind of throw you around! Oh Mike, oh man I'd love that! Oh man I'd get to have my hands all over you! Oh God that would be great!"

"Hey Jamie, here's Jessie's. Still want a cup of coffee, or was that just a ploy?"

"Well – I don't know. If maybe things were a little different, but I guess I've found out what I need to know, so I guess there's not much need for taking your time now."

"Hey come on! I've got time. Just because maybe things aren't going the way you were hoping, that don't mean we can't be friends. Come on, I'll buy!"

"Oh, OK. Yeah thanks! Yeah, got to admit though, like you said, sure ain't going the way I was hoping for!"

"Hey guy, sometimes things go right and sometimes, they stumble! Let's get to know each other anyway. OK? You seem to be a pretty good kind of guy, but you sure do have some strange ways of meeting people."

"Yeah, thanks Mike. I mean, yeah – you could have been a 'real nasty' with me, after what I did."

Mike and Jamie went into Jessie's and took a corner table. A table that was kind of out of the way. Mike offered to buy Jamie a sandwich, or whatever he wanted, since he personally had decided to just have an early supper there, since his wife, Jennifer, and their daughter Sara, were at a Girl Scouts Mother and Daughter dinner, anyway.

After ordering, and sharing some rather useless conversation about nothing in particular, the waitress placed their suppers on the table, and as she walked away, Mike looked at Jamie, and rather quietly asked, "So Jamie, got a partner?"

"No, not anymore. Did for four years, then he, David, decided he wanted somebody that was richer than I am, and he took off with some old guy that could buy him any damn thing he ever wanted."

Then leaning over closer toward Mike, Jamie continued, "Guess sex is not very important to David anymore. Either that, or he sure is not standing true to their relationship. I guess he gets everything paid for from the old guy, and then gets his sex out on the street someplace."

"Well Jamie, if that's the kind of a guy he is, I'm sure you are better off without him."

"Yeah, I know! But I don't like living alone. I'm lonely all the time. I guess that's why I told you what I did at the bus stop. I'm sorry Mike, but man oh man, you are what I'd love to find out there someplace."

"Thank you Jamie! That makes me feel good! Let's face it. Once a guy gets married, he kind of finds out he's out of the 'dating loop,' and hardly ever does anybody tell him he's still 'hot,' as you call it. So I really do appreciate what you've said."

Between bites of his roast beef sandwich and chips that Jamie was enjoying with pleasure, he looked back up at Mike and replied, "Mike my man! Any damn time you don't now if you are hot looking or not, you just give me a call and I sure as the hell, will tell you how damn hot looking you are."

Then leaning over the table and very quietly stating it, Jamie continued, "And I still do want to see you naked. Your old wrestling buddies got to see it, and I want to see it too!"

"Yeah but Jamie, I'm not build like I was when I was like seventeen, eighteen or nineteen. I've gotten older you know."

"Yeah – I know, but you let me decide! I've already told you I like guys older than me, so maybe, to me, you are build better today than you were then." Then, with a very big grin on his face, he looked directly at Mike and added. "You give me the chance – and you let me decide! OK?"

"Jamie, eat your sandwich!"

Looking back again directly at Mike, Jamie picked up part of his sandwich, made a very big grin as if to say, "I'm winning, I'm winning," and he then took a big bite of the sandwich.

With additional patrons coming into the cafe and sitting a little too close to their table, Mike and Jamie drastically changed the tone of their conversation and for the remainder of the dinner they discussed Jamie's job at the photo supply store, and Mike's position with a large PR firm.

As they left the cafe, Jamie again thanked Mike for the sandwich and made a sour-full remark, about his necessity of having to walk, 'all the way home, by himself.'

"O.K. O.K.!" Mike said. "Got any beer at your place?"

"No, I don't, but I sure can grab some on the way if you're coming over to visit for a while."

"Jamie you are a good guy! Jennifer and Sara aren't home for another hour or two anyway, so why not. I've got nothing else to do anyway. Let's stop at Joe's Convenience Place, grab a six pack and then you can show me some of those shots you were telling me about that you took at the Grand Canyon last summer."

Taking off down the street, they only needed to go one block out of their way to stop at Joe's Convenience Place and get the Bud. As they approached Jamie's house, Mike expressed his surprise that it was a house, and not an apartment. Jamie explained that it was the old family residence, and after his mother's death he inherited it, and was in the process of attempting to remodel it, when the money allowed.

After grabbing two Buds, and placing the rest in the refrigerator, the two men went into the living room and rather continued their conversation that had been cut rather short in the cafe when other patrons sat a little too close to their table for that particular conversation.

"O.K. Mike, take your shirt off. I'm not going to rape you, but I want to see what that body looks like. You've shown your body to a lot of people when you hardly had anything on when you were wrestling, you sure as hell can show me what it looks like now."

Shaking his head and kind of grinning, Mike did stand up and pulled his dress shirt out of his waist band, unbuttoned the front, and the cuffs and slowly took it off. His removing it was done so slowly that Jamie started humming the song, "Let Me Entertain You" as he removed it.

"Oh shit man! Damn I knew you were hot! Oh my God Mike, that is so damn hot! Look at that chest and those pecs! Oh Mike, I knew the very first time I saw you that you were one hot built dude! I don't know what you looked like at age eighteen or nineteen but I know damn well you could not have been any hotter then, than you are now! Damn, you have got good biceps! Damn man those are so hot!"

Mike acted rather embarrassed that he was being admired so completely, but internally he did have to admit that the attention and the praise, was very pleasant to hear.

"Hey Mike, let me take some shots of you please? Just your chest and arms, O.K.? I won't put your face in the shots if you don't want, but let me show you what you look like. Can I?"

Slowly, very slowly, Mike finally agreed.

Jamie got his digital camera, well actually one of them, turned some extra lights on is some appropriate places and aimed the camera at Mike.

After each shot, Jamie showed Mike the shot. Mike did have to admit that the shots were turning out rather well, and were looking rather impressive.

"Actually I didn't know I looked like that! I guess looking at yourself in the mirror just doesn't do it, does it?"

After quite a number of shots, and in different positions, Jamie was FINALLY successful in convincing Mike that he really did want some naked shots of him, and that he would show him every shot, just to prove that he was not taking pictures of him with his face showing.

"Never in my greatest imagination did I ever think I would ever be putting myself in a position of where I was taking my pants off and letting some guy take pictures of me naked. Jamie, I don't know about this!"

"Hey Mike, it's all just in fun. Seriously though man. You need to realize just how damn fucking hot of a guy you are! Seriously, you need to see some shots of yourself."

Jamie had worked with other nude men before, taking photo shots of them – the only difference was those men wanted their faces to show in the shots. With Mike, Jamie was being very careful to not show his face, for fear that if he did accidentally, Mike would stop the shoot.

"Hey come on man! Don't hide it! Come on Mike. I know it's getting hard, don't hide it! Hey man, on the bus it was getting hard then too, and I didn't do anything out of line did I? Each time I touched it I could tell it was a little more stiff than the time before. Come on, let it show! It's part of you man, it's part of you!"

"Oh Jamie, Jamie, Jamie! I can not believe you are getting me to do this! Oh shit man! I've never done this before! Shit man, just standing here all naked and having it stick out is enough to make it keep getting harder and harder. Jamie, I'm just not used to being looked at when I'm all undressed."

"Hey man, when you were wrestling, you and the other guys played around some, didn't you? I've always heard of what happens in the locker rooms. Mike, any guy ever grab you?"

"Yeah Jamie, once."

"Well – tell me! What happened?"

"It was after school one day. A group of us were in the locker room and everybody was making bets about what we would or wouldn't do. Well somehow, somebody made a bet that I wouldn't let this guy, by the name of Ralphie, grab my dick. I guess it was all a set up by some of my buddies. I did not know it, but that Ralphie guy liked to suck on dicks. I didn't know the guy, so I didn't know it. Being the smart ass that I was, I of course wanted to win the bet, so I told them that I'd let that Ralphie guy grab me. What I didn't know was that as soon as he grabbed it, he was going to throw his mouth on it and about three other guys were all ready to grab me so that I couldn't pull away from him. Being forced by three guys to let another guy suck me off did kind of get me all excited and I shot off in his mouth. I admit, that at the time, I was kind of pissed, but after I thought about it a lot later, I think I was more pissed that four guys all played a trick on me, more than of what actually happened."

As Jamie listened to Mike talk about his high school experience, he definitely could tell that just the remembering that action was still very exciting to Mike. As Mike talked, and the longer it took for him to relate that experience, his dick kept getting harder and harder. Without actually realizing it, Mike kept moving it and rather playing with it. He kept pushing it down, feeling the strength of it pushing itself back up into an upright position.

"Is that they only time any guy has ever played with you?"

"Yeah, really played with me like that, anyway. I mean, there's been a lot of times when I was wrestling when some guy grabbed my crotch and I really wondered, if the way he was playing with my dick, was really part of his way to wrestle, or was he just playing with me. I remember there were a couple of guys I wrestled with a number of times from another school that really played with it. Well anyway, it sure as hell felt like they were playing with it."

"So what did you do when that happened?"

"I think I usually kind of grabbed them back pretty good whenever I could do it, and get away with it. But I never kept playing with it in my hand like they did with mine. A couple of 'em really took their time letting loose of it. I could tell they were really rolling my balls around in their hands. There was one time though, that I know damn well I grabbed that guy by the nuts and almost did not let go. He grabbed me and it hurt! I know damn well he was into more that just the wrestling, and when it hurt, I really did not care who saw what in the hell was happening. I know by the time I took my hand off of his nuts, he was ready to call the match. I squeezed the hell out of his nuts that day! He didn't act right after that, and I heard his coach ask him what was wrong, but he refused to tell the coach what had happened. I figured he had been caught doing that to other guys before and couldn't admit he did it again. I've always wondered just what kind of sex play that guy is into today! I'm sure he probably only has sex with guys, since I think he's probably too rough to have sex with a gal. I'll bet he is really rough with guys. I hope like hell they give it back to him too!"

"Oh shit man! Oh shit, that has got me so damn hot! Mike, can I get naked too? Do you mind if I get undressed?"

"Shit man. You might as well. Here I am, in your living room, bareassed naked, a raging hard-on sticking out like it hasn't done for years, and me telling you about guys grabbing my dick and how I tried to bust that one guy's nuts in two one day, and also telling you about little Ralphie that sucked me off in the locker room. Shit man! You'd better! Hell man! You've got me all naked, let's see what you look like!"

Jamie quickly shed his shirt, pulled his shoes and socks off, and immediately got rid of the pants. As soon as the pants were gone, it was very damn obvious that he was sexually excited. His stick was standing out a good seven or seven and a half inches, and even Mike looked at it in amazement in how damn thick it was.

"Shit man! You are one fucking hung horse, aren't you?" Mike asked. "Come over here, let me feel that thing!"

Jamie was in complete shock when Mike told him to come over closer so that he could touch his dick. Jamie was in shock, but not so badly that he could not react to the instructions. Mike was lying back on the couch, and Jamie moved over closer so that Mike could grab his dick. Jamie breathed deeply in excitement. The man that had so very shortly earlier, told him he was not gay and did not play around with guys, was now the hunky guy, lying totally nude on his couch, supporting one very, very excited hard-on, and was now reaching out to take his dick in his hand.

As Jamie moved closer, Mike reached out as if not being aware of what he was doing, and took a hold of Jamie's rod. He stroked it back and forth a few times, and then pulled Jamie up even closer. Jamie could see Mike admiring it and realized that his expression on his face was turning into something more deeply rooted that just thinking it was a big and good looking dick. His eyes were glazing at it. His facial expression was turning into to a very deep expression of admiration. Jamie could tell that Mike was looking at his dick as if it was the greatest thing he had ever seen, and his facial expression was an expression of total admiring lust!

Suddenly and without warning, Mike grabbed Jamie's leg, pulled him even closer, raised his head up, and immediately threw his mouth down onto Jamie's rod as far as he possibly could. He took as much of Jamie into his mouth as he possibly could manage. He choked and coughed, but even with that, he attempted to get more and more of Jamie's big rod down in his throat!

"Oh shit man! Oh my God!" Jamie exclaimed as he saw part of his dick disappear into Mike's mouth. "Oh my God Mike! Mike I did not expect you to do that!"

Mike made no response nor attempted any reply except for taking advantage of having Jamie's rod in his mouth and using it for all his might. He kept attempting to take more and more dick, down into his throat, than was even remotely possible.

"Oh! Oh my God man! Oh Mike, suck me, suck me, suck me! Oh yeah man – OH YEAH!!!!" Jamie did actually yell out! Jamie was in complete shock that he was being eaten alive by Mike and Mike's hungry mouth! After Mike had explained that he was a married straight guy, and that the only time that he had ever done anything like this, was that one time when Ralphie had sucked him off, and rather by force, there was no way in hell, that Jamie ever thought this could happen.

Even for Jamie, a guy that was used to having guys suck on his big rod for as long as they could, even he was amazed at how much force and energy Mike was using on taking his dick and eating it as thoroughly as he could. Jamie was standing beside the couch and was being encouraged by Mike's actions, and his hands on Jamie's legs, to face fuck him as much, and as hard as he possibly could. Mike grabbed hold of Jamie's legs and indicated that he wanted him to get up on the couch, straddle his face and feed his dick down into his mouth, by being right on top, and sitting right on his face.

Jamie took the position, and as he pushed as much meat down into Mike's mouth as he possibly could, he continually wondered if Mike had been hiding the real truth and sucked on guys all of the time, or was he maybe finally getting the chance to do something that he had always wanted to do, ever since that day when he got sucked off in the locker room.

Nothing serious was said. Jamie could only says things like "Oh my

God!! Oh God I can not believe this!" And of course, "Oh Mike eat me man! Eat me!"

Mike couldn't say anything. Even if he had needed Jamie to get off of his face, he would have been unable to, since Jamie had so much meat slammed and crammed down into Mike's mouth and into the depths of his throat, that he could not have uttered any words. Jamie just continued to straddle Mike's face and feed him as much of his man stick as he could get Mike to take. And Mike kept trying to take more and more, than what was even possible.

Jamie now realized that everything that was now happening – his sitting directly on Mike's face and strongly force feeding him as much of his thick dick as he could possibly force into Mike's mouth – was all at Mike's desire, and every bit of forcing and ramming that he could do, was completely and totally for Mike's pleasures. He knew he was getting quite rough – very rough, on Mike's face, with the way he was sitting so squarely and firmly on it, and was force feeding his mouth But he also knew that even without saying so, that was what Mike was now wanting and panting for. And, he was obviously wanting it very badly! Jamie was in such a state of shock that, such a very short time ago, this man, the same man that he was now force feeding his telephone pole dick to, claimed to be a straight man that never played with guys.

Jamie just wondered if Mike's remembering back to that day, when he got force sucked, while being held by three other guys as he was sucked off, was what had made him become such a wild animal cock eater. Jamie wondered if, for all of these years, had Mike unknowingly, within him, had this raging desire to do this with some guy, and today finally became the day to let it all happen. Nothing that Jamie could think to do made Mike utter any type of disapproval. Every action and every force that Jamie could force on him, or even in him, was accepted as if Mike was trying to yell, "More! Do More! Do More!"

As Jamie was sitting on Mike's face and force feeding him as much dick as he could manage to get into Mike's mouth, all of a sudden he started yelling, "Oh my God man, I've got to fuck you! Oh Mike I've got to fuck your ass! Oh my God, I've got to fuck you! Oh let me fuck you man! Oh Mike, I want to fuck you! Let me fuck you!"

Mike pushed Jamie off to the side and immediately pulled his mouth off of Jamie's rod, and as if he had just become conscious and in a state of shock, he yelled, "You want what!? You want what!? NO! NO! No, you can't!!"

"Oh Mike, I've got to fuck your ass! Oh, pull your legs up man! Oh let me fuck you man! Let me fuck your ass! I've got to fuck you! Oh man – I've got to fuck your ass!"

You Want What?
Chapter Two:
Calm Down Man

"No, No Jamie! No! Don't fuck me, please! No! Don't! Please, I can't take that!" Mike actually screamed, and attempted to jump up as Jamie told him he just had to fuck his ass.

"O.K., O.K. I won't!" Jamie quickly reassured Mike. "You're O.K., I won't fuck you if you don't want me to. I'm sorry, I'm sorry!"

"Hey Jamie – Jamie I know, inside, mentally, I really do want you to fuck me, but I just can't take it. Jamie, I tried sticking part of a hammer handle up in my ass once, and it just plain hurt too damn bad! Jamie, I wanted to fuck my own ass once, and I just can't take something up in my butt. I'm sorry man, I'm sorry but I know I just can't take it! And besides, for God's sake man, look at the size of the dick you've got on you man! There's no way in hell I could let you fuck me!"

"Hey, hey Mike! Calm down man, I'm not going to fuck you. You're O.K.!"

"Oh thanks man! Thanks!"

As Jamie put Mike's legs back down and then laid down on him and slightly rubbed his sides and his chest to calm him back down, he asked, "So Mike, you tried to fuck yourself with what – a hammer handle once? Is that what you said?"

"Yeah, I did. I didn't think I'd ever have to admit that to anybody, but yeah, I did. It was probably ten or twelve years ago. I was home all by myself and was working in the garage, and I guess I was horny. Anyway, I was just messing around with some stuff in the garage and all of a sudden I wondered what it would feel like to stuff something up in my ass. I was home alone so I knew nobody was going to come in and see what I was doing, so the more I thought about it, the more excited I got, and I dropped my pants and tried to fuck myself with the handle of a hammer. It just didn't work! I tried! I really did, cause the more I thought about it, the more excited I got over wanting to feel something up in there. Jamie, I just couldn't get it up in me, and I thought I was tearing my ass, all up, the way it hurt. I was really excited and I guess I kept trying longer than I should have, and was pushing harder than I should have too."

"Mike, did you use any lube on it? You've got to use some kind of lube on it, especially with something like a hammer handle."

"No, no I didn't! I guess I probably should have, but when I got to thinking about sticking something up in there, I just got all excited and just wanted to see what it would feel like, but then it just plain hurt too bad and I had to quit. I got all excited about fucking myself before I even knew what I was going to use. I looked around for something and that's when I saw the hammer. I thought I could take that. It didn't look too big, but man, it was! Later I kind of wished that I had tried something like maybe the broom handle or something a lot thinner. But then, I was too afraid to try something else. I didn't want it to feel like the handle did and I was afraid that it might!"

As Jamie laid there and softly talked to Mike, he reassured Mike that things could be O.K., and not to always think getting fucked would feel like it did when he tried to fuck his ass with the hammer handle. Then he rather laughed and told Mike he was just glad he had not tried to use the other end of the hammer.

"Mike, seriously, you really needed to use some lube. A hammer handle is not the best thing in the world to start getting fucked by. Really man, I'm not surprised it hurt. Trust me, I'm not going to try and fuck you. You got way too upset when I said I was going to do that, but Mike, you really can get fucked. Guys get fucked all the time. And with dicks bigger than mine!"

"Man, I know I should be able to. I know guys fuck each other all the time, and I guess that's why I got myself so excited that day when I was home all alone and started fantasizing about doing that."

"Mike, have you ever tried to use a dildo on yourself?"

"No! No man, I'm a married guy! I can't have things like dildos around the house. And besides, I'm hardly ever home by myself so that I could even use it."

"But you'd like to if you could, wouldn't you?"

"Yeah – guess I wanted to once, since I did try to do myself that day in the garage, but after that day, and as badly as that hurt, I'm not sure I'll ever try that again."

"Mike, relax, I promise you I'm not going to do anything that you don't want, but I do have some dildos, and when you decide you might want to see if you can take one up in your hot little ass, I've got a small one that you can start with."

"Hey Jamie, thanks man. Seriously when you got all excited and told me you needed to fuck me, I do admit I got really scared. I don't know if I'll ever try putting something back up in my butt again, but let me decide that later. O.K.? Hey, for now, can you just kind of lick on me and maybe suck on my dick a little. I've got to admit, when you got all excited and said you had to fuck me, I kind of all freaked out. Jamie, I need to calm back down. Let's face it, man. When I left the office today, I sure as hell never expected to be doing what I'm doing now, so I need to take things kind of slow. O.K.?"

"Hey man, I understand. Really I do. Just lie there and let me take care of you. You're O.K., I'm just going to lick you, taste you, rub you and put that dick of yours in my mouth and suck real hard, on it. Maybe after I suck on you for awhile, then maybe your ass will get all anxious to try something up in there again."

"Yeah Jamie, play with me for awhile. Seriously man, I'm not sure about putting anything up in my butt today. For some reason, I feel like I need to think about doing that for some time, and then maybe decide later if I can do it or not. O.K.?"

"Hell yes man! Hell yes!" Jamie quickly replied as he looked up at Mike's face, just moments before he impaled his mouth with Mike's beef steak. "Hell yes man! From the way you are now talking, I'm getting the idea that maybe, just maybe, tonight is not going to be the last time you come to visit me, right?"

As Mike laid back and enjoyed the feeling of Jamie on top of him, and the feeling of Jamie's hands rubbing up and down his body line, and noticing also the warm breath hitting his stomach as Jamie approached his raging hard-on, he answered. "Well man, it's up to you. I'll admit, I sure as hell never expected to be doing this tonight, but Jamie, the more you play with me and feel me, the more excited I am about being here. I've never, never, told anybody else about getting sucked off in that locker room that day, and I sure as hell, have never told anybody about me trying to fuck my own ass with that hammer handle. So I guess now I feel like I've pretty well given you all of me, and now I feel like I've got me a new friend, like none that I've ever had before. Jamie, I admit, I've wanted to play with some guy for a long time now, or at least wanted to find out what it was like, but things just never worked out where I could. I'm glad, really glad, you told me there at the bus stop that you wanted to suck my cock, or whatever it was you said. Shocked the shit out of me at the time, but thank God you had the guts to do it. This is feeling good."

Jamie looked up at Mike, smiled and said. "Mike, that makes me feel good! And, I'm damn glad you took it O.K., and didn't get pissed at me. If I had known earlier that you had been wanting to see what playing with a guy was like, it sure as hell would not have taken me two weeks to get around to telling you I wanted to play with you. So I'm the first guy you've ever played with, I assume, or – are there still things to tell?" Jamie asked as he looked up at Mike, grinned a large smile and then immediately placed the back of his throat and his tonsils on Mike's rod.

"Oh man! Oh Jamie – the more you do that, the more I'm just fucking melting. Yeah – you are right. I could tell from the way you asked that last question – you know damn well that dick's been sucked on by other guys, don't you?"

Without taking Mike's dick out of his mouth, Jamie tipped his head up so he could look into Mike's eyes, and just grunted a 'Yeah' as he attempted a mouthful of cock smile at Mike. He then uttered, "Tell me, tell me."

"Jamie I've never had it as nice as I'm getting it tonight. I've never been in some guy's house where I could lie down and let him lie on top of me like this. All of my previous blow jobs have been in the car, in the bed of some guys old rattle pickup truck, or in some dark alley, some damn dirty place where, with some guy that probably didn't even have a home, could kneel down in front of me, grab my crotch, open my pants and take my dick like he hadn't had anything to eat in days. Every blow job I've ever had, well except for Ralphie and the locker room, has been in some dark and stinking place where I had to keep watching for cars to come by, hoping that some cop didn't drive by right then. I've wanted to do it like this for years and years, but tonight is the first time I've ever gotten to. Jamie, this is nice, real nice! Real nice!"

Jamie listened to Mike tell about his prior experiences, and as he did he managed to eat even that much more of Mike's stiff stick, and actually feel that what was then happening was really a little more than just sucking and having sex. He was really feeling a sharing of a true love, being expressed by Mike in the way he was describing his prior times. Jamie was feeling very good that he had managed to gain enough courage, to tell Mike that he wanted to suck on him.

Jamie pulled off of Mike's dick and slid his face up Mike's stomach line, and slowly slid his face over so that his lips were now directly on Mike's right nipple.

"Oh yeah man! Oh yeah!" Mike almost yelled as he watched and felt Jamie place his mouth on his tit. "Oh Yeah – oh man that feels so damn good! Oh man, yeah suck on my tit!"

With that encouragement, Jamie took Mike's right nipple into his mouth and so very slightly bit down, just a little. Remembering Mike's fear of getting it up in the ass, Jamie did not want to freak Mike out by biting too hard.

He really did want Mike to ask for it, and he did.

"Oh yeah, chew on my tit! Oh man, please, please chew on it, please!"

Jamie reacted to the instruction and not only chewed on it, but he sucked it very strongly, and then, as he released the strong suck, he bit firmly. Mike jumped and jerked, but he did not tell Jamie to stop. He just grunted and groaned a very accepting grunt, and he grabbed Jamie around the chest and squeezed. Jamie took that as a signal of O.K., and also maybe a signal to move over to the left tit.

As Jamie placed his mouth on Mike's left tit, Mike grabbed hold of Jamie and squeezed him very tightly. "Yes man yes! Oh yes bite my tit! Bite me man, bite me! I like that ! I like that! Oh my God Jamie, I like that! I've never felt that before! Do me some more! Oh Jamie that is feeling so good. Man, I've never felt that before. Jamie, that's the first time I've ever been chewed on, and you probably won't believe me, but tonight's the first time I've ever sucked on some guy's cock. Jamie, you are the first guy I've ever sucked on. You're the first guy to ever put his dick in my mouth. I've been sucked on probably fifteen or twenty times, but I've never sucked on some other guy until I did you tonight. Seriously man, when you dropped your pants and I saw that dick, I about went out of my mind wanting to suck on it. I've never felt that way before. I've never really ever wanted to suck on some guy. I've always wanted him to just suck me off and then let me go. I've always figured that I was wanting to relive that day in the locker room when I was held down so that Ralphie could suck on me. I guess that was more exciting to me than what I wanted to admit, wasn't it? When I grabbed you and pulled you toward me and put my mouth on your dick, I didn't know for sure what I was doing, but I knew I had to do it! I just kind of spaced out knowing that I had to put your dick in my mouth and in as far as I could get it. Jamie, I was kind of possessed. The sight of your dick made me kind of go crazy – until I heard you say that you needed to fuck me. Then all of a sudden, I guess I kind of snapped out of it and came to. Really before that, I felt like I was someplace else. Felt good, but kind of, out there, so to say. I guess my mind just went kind of crazy just wanting to feel your cock in my mouth for a little while. Man, I've never felt that way before! Oh Jamie, this is so good! Man, this is good! I just don't understand me, but this is good!"

You Want What?
Chapter Three:
Let's Get on the Floor

As Jamie laid there on top of Mike, kissing his tits and rubbing his hands up and down the sides of Mike's body, Mike was returning the great feelings by hugging Jamie and giving his body major tight squeezes as he kissed his neck and his face.

"Oh Mike man, oh that feels so good when you squeeze me like that! Oh that feels so good to me!"

"Hey guy. You feel damn good to me too! Suck my cock man – suck my cock."

"Yeah, this is feeling so damn good. Mike, I've got to admit, you sure are turning out to be a hell of a lot more fun and exciting than just some hot built guy that I found at a bus stop. Really man, this is one hell of a lot better than just getting to suck some stranger off, and that's all I was hoping for at first!"

Having stated that comment of admiration, Jamie immediately moved down and took all of Mike's rod in his mouth and sucked on it with vim and vigor. As his mouth was completely involved in taking care of Mike's man-meat stick, his hands continued a body roaming of major proportions.

"Oh man, oh!" Mike groaned and moaned as he enjoyed the feeling of Jamie's strong masculine hands moving all around his body, and his realization that he was finally in the position that he had dreamed about for so long. On his back, a man lying on top of him, both being completely naked, and his seven inch rod firmly placed into his playmate's mouth as far and as firmly as he could possibly place it. He was lying down, a hot hunk was on top, and he was getting sucked off! He was being taken care of, completely!

"Jamie, Jamie! Hey, let's get on the floor so I can suck on you too. O.K.? I want to suck on you while you are sucking on me, O.K.?"

With that suggestion sounding quite nice to Jamie, he released Mike's pole from his mouth, and he helped Mike up from his prone position. The two men immediately positioned themselves on the floor, and of course neatly placed themselves on the thick area rug, rather than on the bare hardwood surface. Mike faced north as Jamie laid down headed south.

With neither man really knowing for sure just who was expected to be on his back, and then of course having the other man lying on top, both men took a position of lying on his side. Neither man suggested which position he felt they should take. Actually neither man had his mouth empty long enough to make any suggestions. Immediately and as quickly as they were beside each other on the floor, they were both eating cock.

Jamie's enormous rod was still a problem for Mike to take completely, and especially now that it was harder and stiffer than even earlier, but he managed very successfully, and especially well for a mouth that had never tasted a man's meaty rod, before this day.

Jamie swallowed all of Mike's stick and with the strong sucking action that he was giving it, Mike thought perhaps Jamie was now trying to stretch it longer than it actually was. As his hands were quickly floating the entire length of Mike's hot body, Jamie rolled his hot and anxious sex partner over, onto his back, so that he could force his mouth down, and onto, that beautiful piece of meat, that he wanted swallowed down inside of his throat, as far, and as quickly as possible. Mike knew immediately that Jamie was forcing his mouth down onto his meat with as much force and energy as he could muster. And he was enjoying it. He was finally getting treated the way he wanted. This was not dark alley sex! This was true male to male sex, and he was enjoying all of it. In-fact, he had more to enjoy, than he could get in his mouth!

Mike was totally engrossed with his own actions of just trying to take all of Jamie into his mouth when very unexpectedly he felt a new feeling down around the area of his body, where earlier he had admitted, that he had attempted to force that hammer handle, some years ago.

He knew Jamie was feeling his ass. He could feel Jamie's fingers. He could feel Jamie's hand feeling around down there. He had a big mouthful of Jamie's cock, and could not say anything. He froze in his actions and his movements. Jamie sensed that Mike had frozen. He sensed that Mike was starting to get scared, and he knew that having his hand, and his finger tips, right at Mike's asshole was making Mike very nervous.

"Hey man, everything is O.K.!" Jamie reassured Mike as he pulled off of Mike's steel rod, stiff dick, only long enough to let him know that nothing, nothing was going to happen that Mike did not approve of, or maybe even ask for.

"Lie back man! You are O.K. I'm just kind of rubbing that sweet spot back there making sure it's O.K., and nothing is going to go on, that you don't want. I'll just rub it and kind of love on it like I'm doing to your dick. I've just got my mouth on your dick, and my hand on your ass! O.K.? O.K.?"

Mike attempted to kind of shake his head, 'Yes,' to indicate he heard what Jamie had said, and then both men went back to the 'cock-in-the-mouth' sucking that had been kind of, shortly, disrupted.

Slowly and carefully Jamie continued the ass rubbing and at the same time listening very carefully for any sounds of displeasure that Mike might make. He heard none. He forcefully, and rather roughly, sucked on Mike's rod, somewhat in an attempt to distract Mike's attention away from his ass area, so that he could maybe make a little more progress back there without Mike actually realizing what was really going on.

The progress was moving along very well. Jamie sensed that his forceful action on Mike's dick was allowing him to do a little more, and again – even a little more – in Mike's asshole area. One finger slid in, and Mike only made a very slight movement, as his most private and sensitive body part was being slightly opened and entered. Jamie played with his one finger, as if this was the first asshole that he had ever entered. He watched and listened for Mike to object.

Jamie then asked. "Hey man, you O.K.? I've got a finger up in your ass, you know?"

"Yeah, I know. Yeah, I felt it go in. I'm O.K.! Kind of wiggle it a little so I can feel it, O.K.?"

Jamie reacted to the request and he knew he was starting to be successful in getting Mike to relax and realize that his ass could be played with, and without any real pain.

"You like that? That feel good?"

"Yeah, that feels pretty good. You just got one finger in there?"

"Yeah, I do now. Want me to put another one in?"

"Yeah I do, I think I do anyway! Yeah, yeah I do. I know I do, but I'm afraid to admit it. I don't want it to hurt like it did that day in the garage. Try and see if I can take it."

As Jamie got up from his position on the floor, he told Mike, "Hey man. Lie still. I'll be right back. This is going good, and I'm going to get some lube so that I can get my fingers good and slippery before we go any farther. O.K.?"

Knowing that Jamie was now wanting to put his fingers up in his ass, he simply knew that pretty soon Jamie was going to want to put that damn big rod of his up in there, instead of just his fingers, and Mike just knew there was no way in hell that he could get that damn big dick of Jamie's up in his butthole.

"Yeah O.K.!" Mike replied as he laid there and watched Jamie head down the hallway toward the bedroom.

As Jamie departed, of course bareassed and showing all of his positive parts, Mike thought to himself. 'Damn shit man! He has got one hell of a hot ass! I hadn't looked at that yet! Shit man! God man, that is nice! Fuck, I've never played with some other guy's ass before, but shit man, damn man, that one is fucking hot!'

As Jamie returned and started to lie back down, he coated his fingers with the KY that he brought back with him, and he heard Mike saying. "Damn man! You have got one hot fucking looking ass. Jamie, I hadn't looked at your ass real well until I watched you walking down the hall and your shinny bare butt was shining back at me! Shit man! With the fuckin' dick you've got and an ass like that! Shit man! You are one hot stud, aren't you?"

Jamie looked at Mike, smiled widely and offered. "Hey thanks man! Not as hot as yours, but thanks anyway. It likes to be fingered you know. If you think it looks hot, you need to put a finger or two up in it and then see how hot it is. Here, put some KY on your fingers, and I'm going to let you finger fuck me, while I play with your ass. O.K.?"

"Oh shit yes man, hell yes! Oh Jamie! I never, and I do mean never, had the lust for looking at some other guy's ass or ever thought about wanting to play with one until I saw you walking down that hall. Shit man! What in the hell is happening to me tonight? God man! I've never sucked on some guy's dick until tonight and now your ass has got me all hot and bothered. Yeah man, yeah! I want to play with that ass! How many fingers can I shove up in there?"

"Well, maybe shove, is the wrong phrase, but if you go slow, I'm sure you will find enough room to get at least four fingers up in there and if I'm in the right position, you could loose your whole damn hand up in there."

"Oh my God Jamie! Jamie, my whole hand? Oh shit man! Jamie, seriously, you've never had some guy's whole hand up in your ass before have you?"

"Hey, what can I say? Some of us horny guys like to do funny things once in awhile. Well – kind of like maybe trying to put a hammer handle up our ass without any lube on it. Right?"

"Other words – you are saying, yes – you have had a hand up in your ass. Right?"

Jamie rather grinned at Mike and replied. "Well, yeah. A few times."

"Oh God Jamie!! God man! Didn't that hurt like hell? How many times have you done that?"

"Hey the hurt, well that's something you need to expect, so you've really got to want it done, or you of course, don't do it. For some reason guys

– well guys like me – that get fisted, are for some reason the kind of a guy that likes to hit the limits. Mike, I really don't know why, but letting some guy put his hand up inside of my ass is a real mental turn on to me. Sure, the ass is full and feels good, especially after he's got his fist up in there, but for some funny reason, it's the mental thing more than the ass thing. Letting some guy do me that way, is a real fucking turn on! It's like giving my whole body to him, and letting him do to it whatever he wants. It's letting him completely take me and have total control over me. It's showing him what I can do for him. I think it has something to do with my childhood."

"What do you mean? Your childhood? Why do you say that?"

"Oh, I don't know! I guess when I was a kid, I never felt like I was one of 'the guys,' so to say. I always felt left out. Never one of the kids that was always praised for doing good stuff. So anyway, I guess now I do stuff that I figure those guys can't do. Of course, what I do is pretty private, but I'd still like to have some of them walk in the room sometime when I'm getting fisted and just ask 'em, 'Hey man – can you do this?' "

"Oh man! Wow! Well, I guess I can see what you mean. Childhood wasn't the greatest for you, I assume?"

"Assume? Hell man, there's no assuming about it! I was not the basketball jock, not the baseball jock, not the football jock and of course not the wrestling jock like you were, so I was not the prize of my school – I guess you could say!"

"Well, let me tell you something right here and right now! You might not have been the prize of your school, but you sure are the prize as far as I'm concerned! You are one fucking hot dude, and what in the hell those other guys turned out like, I don't know, but I will tell you that someday, and someday soon, I hope, I am going to be the latest guy to find my fist stuck up in that hot little ass of yours, and I'm with you when I say I'd love for some of those guys to walk in on us and watch you suck my hand right up in your butt!"

"Oh shit man, oh shit! You mean it Mike? I mean – you plan on fisting me? Really man, you'd do that? You'd fist me?"

"Hell yes I do, and I would! If you'll let me, I'd be happy as hell to do it. If that will show you how much of a man you are, sure I will. And besides, the whole idea of my hand up inside of you is a major, major, hot turn on! I never thought about doing that to some guy before, but now that the idea of, 'my hand up in your ass,' is being talked about, damn man, hell yes I want to! Shit man! When I watched that butt of yours going down that hall, I wondered just why in the hell it was as hot as it is, and maybe that's the reason! If getting fisted, as you call it, is what makes an ass look that damn hot, then maybe I need to start that direction!"

"Oh shit man! Oh God Mike, I like they way things are headed here! Let's go one step at a time, and see just where it leads. O.K.? I'm going to play with this ass back here, but I sure as hell am not planning on fisting it tonight, so I guess that does mean tonight is not going to be our last night playing – right?"

"Shit no man! Jamie, when I headed out of the office today, I had no reason in hell to think that my life was going to change before I got home tonight. That one statement that you made at the bus stop, 'I want to suck your cock,' sure is changing a lot of things for me. I don't know man. If it happened to be some other guy, maybe things would not be turning out this way, but Jamie, with you, this is fucking heaven. Heaven man! Heaven! Come on, get your fingers in my ass, and let me get my fingers in your ass. But hey man, remember, my ass still needs some serious loving before you go ramming too much up in there. I'm still fucking nervous about putting stuff up in there, but Jamie, I completely trust you and even if I scream or something, I really do want you to finger me and maybe try to get all four fingers up in me tonight, if at all possible. O.K.?"

"Hell yes that's O.K.! Shit man, earlier I was pretty damn sure I wasn't even going to get to kiss that ass, the way you freaked out when I told you I wanted to fuck you. Hell man, now you are letting me finger it? Shit man, this is unbelievable!"

"How many fingers do you want me to stick up in you?"

"Hey, like that ole saying goes, 'Give till it hurts!' When you've got too much up in there, I'll let you know. O.K.?"

"Oh shit yeah, and then I'll get to kiss it if it hurts, right?"

"Hell yes you can man! In fact, here! Spread your legs so I can get my face in there! Yeah man – kiss my ass and I'll kiss yours too!"

"Oh Mike, you'll like this! I'm sure you never imagined earlier today you'd have your face stuck up in some guy's ass, licking his butt tonight, did you?"

You Want What?
Chapter Four:
Unbelievable

"Oh Jamie, this is fucking unbelievable! I never thought I'd get a chance to enjoy something this great. Kiss my ass man, kiss my ass!"

Jamie sure did not need the instructions to place his face squarely, in place, right at Mike's ass opening. He was licking and kissing all the spots he could get his tongue close to, just hoping that Mike would treat his ass the same. And the idea was working. Mike was using every bit of skin back there to his excitement.

"Finger me man, finger me!" Mike stated very urgently. His anxiety was definitely changing from his former, 'keep your hands away from my butt' ideas. Jamie did and lost no time in doing what Mike wanted.

"Yeah, do me too! Yeah Mike, finger me, put your hand up in my ass man, yeah finger my hole!"

Mike and Jamie completely removed themselves from the real world as they became completely engrossed in each other and each other's bodies.

Silence fell over the room as each man explored and roamed all of the exciting parts of his floor mate. For an extended period of time, the two acted as if they were one. One movement in one directions, immediately was followed with an accompanying move to complement the feeling and the tasting as well as the deep exploring that was now is rapid session.

"Oh Mike stick you hand up in my ass man, put your hand in my ass!"

Somewhat shocked, and rather dumbfounded by hearing the request, Mike immediately replied, "Oh Jamie no. I can't do that! No man, that will hurt you! No man, no don't make me do that. No not tonight! I've got to get used to that idea first man. Jamie, let's not go there tonight, O.K.? Let's maybe just do some dildo stuff so that I can really learn that getting it in the butt is not as bad as I keep thinking it is. O.K.?"

"Yeah, of course it's O.K. Mike. Mike, I just keep forgetting that you still have those old, bad, deep, dark, fears about stuffing stuff up in the ole asshole, since you tried to tear your own ass out once, so yeah, let me get the dildos and let's have some fun with them, O.K.? Sucking on your dick and either playing with your butt some or you playing with mine some will be perfect. I'll be a happy camper. Lie still, I'll be right back!"

Jamie jumped up and headed for his storage drawer of 'fun toys.' In just a minute he returned with three dildos in hand.

"Oh shit man, you're not planning on putting that stuff up in me are you?" Mike almost cried as he looked at the 'hardware' that Jamie had just brought back in with him.

"Hey relax man, relax. This one is the starter. It's really skinny and goes up and in real easy. Even in an ass slammed shut as tight as yours is right now, it's going to feel good. Mike, once you find out how this one gets you all turned on, once it's up inside of you, then we'll move up to the next one, just a little thicker and a little longer, and then by the time you've loved on that one up in your ole butthole for a few minutes, then you will really be begging me to put this eighteen incher in and see just how much of it we can make disappear up in there."

"Jamie I'm telling you man, I'm trusting you, but I'm still fucking nervous about anything going up in my ass!"

"Hey man, everything is going to be O.K. Here Mike, lie down here and you just let me take care of your hot looking ass for a little bit and I'm sure you are going to be wishing you had done this a long time ago."

Jamie had Mike lie down on his gut and spread his arms up and out some so that he could get Mike into a very relaxed position. He lubed the small dildo up well with some KY and then shot some right at Mike's ass. He used the time of spreading that KY around on Mike's butt to also do a little more fingering, and noticing that as he slid one finger in, Mike's ass moved in a very encouraging way, and then as he slid the second finger in, he heard Mike actually utter an encouragement of, "Yeah, yeah." Softy and very quietly, but none the less, he was moving in that direction and not telling Jamie to pull his fingers out.

Jamie took the skinny dildo and placed it right beside the fingers he had up in Mike's butt. As he pulled his fingers out, he started sliding the dildo in. He knew Mike would tell something was happening back there. Mike rather squirmed and moved, but then Jamie realize that Mike was giving off all of the right sounds to indicate he was taking the dildo without trouble. Slowly, very slowly, Jamie continued the journey up and into Mike's butt. One inch in, two inches in, three inches in, and Mike was still doing O.K.

"Hey man, how you doing?" Jamie asked as he rubbed Mike's hot ass with his left hand, and his right hand held the dildo in place.

"I'm O.K. I can tell you've got something up in me. I can feel it – but I'm O.K."

"Good man, good. You just lie there and relax. I'm having some fun back here. You're doing good – doing real good."

Jamie continued his entrance into Mike's ass and as he got past the number four and then the number five and then the six inches, he again asked Mike how he was doing.

"Good man I'm doing good. Jamie I can feel that up in there and yeah, got to admit, it's feeling pretty good. How much you got up in me?"

"Oh just part of it man, not too much yet!" Jamie replied, as he didn't really want to tell Mike that he already had six or seven inches up in him. He wanted to wait until Mike had taken at least ten or eleven inches up in his ass before Jamie let him know how much was up in there.

As the dildo continued to move on up into Mike's butt, Jamie could certainly tell that Mike was now starting to move more to the direction of wanting it and actually trying to get his butt to suck on it to bring more of it up and in himself.

"O.K. man, how's that feeling? How's your butt now?"

"Hey Jamie, you sure are right! It's feeling good. I guess maybe I was a fool for thinking something that skinny was going to hurt. How much you got up in me – what four or five inches?"

"Well Mr. Mike, this dildo is only about fourteen inches long, and right now there is only about four inches of it sticking out the ass end of you, so I guess you must have about ten inches of dildo stuck up in your butt right now man!"

"Oh my God man! Ten inches!!? Jamie, really I can't have ten inches of that up in me do I? Oh shit man, are you sure?"

"Yip I am. Here tell you what. I'm going to put my finger on the dildo right at your asshole and then pull it out and show you what was up in your ass, O.K.?"

Jamie placed his finger on the dildo right at Mike's ass and pulled it out and then showed it to Mike.

"O.K. man, that's the part that you had up in your ass. Felt pretty damn good didn't it?"

"Oh shit Jamie, I can't believe that! I took that much up in my ass?"

"Yes, yes you did, and it felt pretty damn good didn't it?"

"Yeah, I've got to admit it did. Really Jamie, I thought you probably had about four or five inches up in me. Man oh man! I never figured I took that much. Where in the hell did it go? Man, I can't believe that!"

"O.K. man, moving on! That was 'Mr. Skinny.' Now – time to move on to one just a little more meaty. This one is just a little fatter, so we'll have some more fun here. You're O.K. with this all now, right?"

"Shit man I guess so. Really I still can't believe I took that much of the other one. I guess if I can take ten inches of that one, then I should be able to take some of this one. It's not too much fatter is it? Don't look too much fatter."

"No, it's not much thicker. That skinny one I think is about four inches around and this one is only about five or five and half, so it's not that much bigger. Lie down and relax. I'm having fun back here. Here, here, tell you what. Flip over. Lie on your back and let me put this up in you and suck on your cock at the same time, O.K.?"

"Oh shit Jamie, God this is so fucking hot to me! I'm starting to relax some now that you've shown me I can take something up in my butthole without it tearing me all apart. Yeah, I guess I'm getting relaxed. I'm starting to kinda get really anxious for you to start that one up in me."

And so Jamie did. He had Mike put his knees up so that his ass was nicely exposed and after doing some good and ample lubing of the dildo and the ass area – once again accomplished with some finger foreplay – he placed the tip of the dildo right at Mike's hole. "Ready man? Ready?"

"Yeah man, yeah I am. Yeah Jamie, let me feel that."

Jamie opened the hole and pushed the tip in.

"Oh shit man! Oh man yeah I can feel that! Oh man, that feels one hell of a lot thicker than it looks like. Oh Jamie, let me relax on it a minute."

Jamie let the dildo just sit there with about one inch up in Mike's ass, and he bent over and took Mike's stiff cock rod into his mouth. As he sucked and rather moved Mike's attention to his dick rather than his ass, Jamie slowly and very carefully slid another three, four, five and then six more inches of the dildo up into Mike's ass.

Looking up at Mike, Jamie asked. "How you doing man, how you feeling?"

"Good, I'm feeling good! You've got more of that up in me now don't you? I can tell you've moved it up in me some haven't you?"

"Yeah, yeah. I've been slightly pushing on it as I sucked the sweet juices out of that rod of yours! Damn man, what a dick and what an ass and all of the rest of you. I hope like hell your wife appreciates this body as much as I do! Does she lick you like I do?"

"Hey man, remember, I'm married! The honeymoon is over! It's called living the married life now. An occasional fuck in the hay once in awhile, then flip over and go to sleep. Jamie, after a few years with the old wedding ring around your finger, nights like this just don't happen at home any more. This is the hottest sex I've experienced in years! Honest man, this is great. But Jamie, I don't know what time it is, but I know I had better be hitting the road or I am going to have to try and explain way too much if I get home after she and Sara does. Use that dildo on me for just a little longer, see how much of it I can easily take, then I've got to get out of here. We've got to make some plans for when I can come back over here and get the real thing."

"Yeah I was wondering about that too!" Jamie replied. "Just lie there and relax, you've already got about seven inches of this up in you, let me see if I can slide some more up in there."

With Mike's encouragement, and some rather animated ass actions, Jamie slid another three inches of the dildo up into Mike's ass before Mike told him he thought maybe that was going to be as far as he could go.

"Yeah man, I think that's the limit. I can feel it pushing on something up in there. Maybe the next time, we can see if I can do more, but for now, I think I've been fucked as much as I can do. It's O.K. if I come back another night and let you do the real fucking then, right?"

"Shit, hell yeah man! Yeah man, yeah! I'm glad we made the progress tonight that we did. Lie back there a minute and let me finish sucking you off before I pull this dildo out of your ass and you jump up. You need to cum man, and I need the protein. If I don't blow you off before you get dressed, you'll probably have cum marks all over those dress slacks!"

With that statement, Mike laid back, Jamie once again got Mike's rod into this throat and within about one minute of fast and furious sucking, Mike was yelling. "Oh God Jamie! Oh Jamie I'm about ready to cum! Oh man, oh man! Oh shit Jamie this feels fucking good! Suck me, suck me!!! Oh Jamie, I'm cummmmin man, I cummmin! Oh shit man! Oh man what a feeling!! Oh shit, it feels different when you cum and you've got something stuck up in your ass don't it? Oh man, I never felt that before! Shit man, that was great!"

As Jamie licked his lips and wiped the cum, that was now dripping off of the end of his chin, he looked at Mike, smiled, and said. "Hey the young kid can show the older man some new stuff, I guess!"

"Oh God yes man, I guess so! Jamie this has been great! I sure did not know cummin could feel so good and so different, just because you've got something stuffed up in your butt! Man, thanks for that! Wow! Wow!"

Jamie slowly started pulling the dildo out, and as it snapped out, Mike asked Jamie to show him just how much of the 'dick' he had taken up in his ass.

"Oh shit man, I took that much!? Wow! Man I never thought I'd ever do that, and on top of that, I'm shocked like hell right now that I want more. Jamie, you sure have proven to me tonight that getting my ass fucked and stuffed is the way to go. Shit man, I wish I had been doing this for years now, but hey – better late than never, so they say. Jamie, when can I come back? I want to feel that rod of yours up in my ass! I need to get back over here just as soon as possible!"

You Want What?
Chapter Five:
Damn Your Ass is Good

Mike's evening with the dildos going up in his ass, and his final realization that even maybe a fucking telephone pole stuck up in there just might be fun too, made him more than overly anxious to get back over to Jamie's place and let that young man finally show him what it feels like to have a man lying on his back, and sticking his stiff hard rod up in his ass.

Jamie and Mike had decided that 'somebody-up-above' was on their side since Jennifer and Sara were going to be gone to some kind of a regional Girl Scout function over the week-end, and that would give Mike some good 'open' time that he could easily spend with Jamie. Mike told Jamie that they were headed out for Seattle, right after school was out on Friday, and that they would even be gone by the time he got home from work. It was quickly decided that they would now share an additional bus ride home together, but their ride on Friday would definitely be a little different than the one they had experienced that day.

"Hey man, I was getting kind of worried here that something was holding you up and maybe you were not going to get here on time."

Mike looked at Jamie, shook his head some, and replied. "Yeah, I know! Whenever you want to made damn sure you do something specific, that is when the whole day falls apart on you. I got involved in some crap at the office, but thankfully I managed to push it off on Frank, right at the last minute.

Sorry I made you worry."

"Hey no problem now. You're here, I'm here and thank goodness the bus is late. I'm usually pissed when it's late, but today I'm glad," Jamie said, as he looked Mike over very animatedly, so that Mike knew what was happening.

"Jamie, stop that! Somebody's going to see you doing that and wonder just what in the hell is going on!"

"I know, I know! But Mike, it's been four days since I finally got you all stripped down and naked, and right now I'm just kind of undressing you with my eyes, getting myself all anxious for us to be spending the evening together."

"Well let me tell you something young man, so am I! Hey, here comes the bus. Now keep your hands off of me while we are on the bus, or I will have a fucking hard-on like none you have ever seen before! O.K.?"

Jamie looked at Mike, laughed and said, "Yeah – yeah! Maybe, maybe!"

Just as he said "Maybe," the bus stopped and the door opened. Mike and Jamie got on the bus, and immediately Jamie managed to re-play the entire previous bus ride as if it had never happened before.

As Mike and Jamie got off at 83rd Street, Mike grabbed Jamie buy the shoulder and jokingly shook him. "Damn man, I told you to keep your hands to yourself. I've got a raging hard-on right now that is visible from downtown, I'm sure!"

"Good! That's good man, that's good. Nobody saw anything, anyway, did they? I don't think they did, did they?"

"Jamie, I'm not too sure. That once, when you reached back and really took a hold of me big time, I'm not so sure that kid sitting in the seat beside me didn't see that!"

"Oh that college like kid?"

"Yeah, that kid. You grabbed me and then when I looked over his way, he was looking up at me and was grinning like some big wild army cat. I really don't know for sure cause I wasn't looking at him when you did that, but right after that, he sure did act like he knew something."

"Good! I mean, that might be good! He was the one with the red t-shirt on?"

"Yeah that kid."

"Shit man, he was hot. I saw him. Hell, I wish I had known that maybe he saw that! He grinned after that, uh? We just may need to keep our eyes open for that guy on the bus then. He could be fun! Shit man, he was kind of hot!"

The two men made the walk to Jamie's house with a lot of goofing and joking around, and it was very obvious that neither man was going to be taking any extra time getting ready for some hot, gay guy, bareassed, skin to skin sex, once they got in the door.

As they closed the front door, Jamie immediately grabbed Mike, flung him around, placed his right hand squarely on Mike's now major hard-on, and threw his left hand around Mike's body and grabbed his ass.

"Come on man, I want some of this, and I want it now!"

Mike and Jamie headed for the bedroom, letting clothes fly as they went down the hall, and within actually seconds, both men were naked and on the bed.

"Jamie my man, this time there is not going to be any of that stupid stuff about me being afraid of getting something up in my ass! I've had those dildos of yours up in there, and now I want you up in there. I'm serious, I've been so fucking horny for this ever since I left here the other night, I've been having trouble keeping my mind on work and other stuff. I feel like some teenage girl that's finally getting to go out with the hunk of the school. Fuck me man, and I mean fuck me good and hard!!"

"Holy shit man! Have I got the same guy in here that I had the other night?" Jamie joked and laughed. "Man oh man! You sure as hell are ready today, aren't you? God Mike, what a fucking change! Give me that ass, let me at it!"

This time there was no waiting and definitely no foreplay. Mike wanted it, and he wanted it then – RIGHT THEN!

"Put that dick of death up in me man, fuck me!"

It sure did not require a second request for Jamie to throw his body down across Mike's hot muscular body, grab his hard-on dick, and after smearing only a small amount of KY on Mike's ass, he pushed it in.

"Oh my God yes man! Oh yes! Oh Jamie, God man I never thought having something like your big thick stiff dick stuck up in my ass could ever feel so damn good! Oh man, I am so sorry that I screamed, telling you to not fuck me, and I'm sorry that I ever, even, said that. Oh man your dick sure is nothing like that fucking hammer handle I tried to use on me once. Oh man – push on me – yeah push in hard! Oh God yes – oh yeah man, push on my ass hard!!!"

"Hey getting it in the ass ain't so bad after all is it Mike? When I told you I wanted to suck on you, I sure never figured that simple suck was going to turn into anything like this! Man you were fucking ready for this today, weren't you? Shit man, you sure have changed your mind about putting something up in there, haven't you? Your ass is hot – fucking hot man – fucking hot!! I know now why those high school guys liked to wrestle with you and grab you. Shit man – all of you is one hot fucking guy!! You are one hot fuck! Oh shit man, I sure as hell did not think that I'd be this deep in you within, what, four minutes of being in the house? Shit man, I'm surprised you didn't grope me on the bus, instead of me grabbing you! God this is good!"

"Jamie I wish like hell now that I had never tried fucking myself with that damn hammer handle. Ever since that day, I've really fought against the idea of letting any guy get close to my ass, and I have missed out on this for years now, because of that. I thought that last dildo you put up in me felt good, but God man, your dick is out of this world! Does doing the fucking feel as good as being the one down here and letting you fuck me like this?"

"Oh hell yeah, man. Yeah. Different feeling I know, but man getting to lie on top of something like you and an ass like yours has got to be good! Hell, even if I was just lying here and didn't have my cock rammed up in your butt, it would be great, but getting to stick it up in you and letting your ass grab a hold on it, is fucking good! Squeeze your ass! Yeah man! Yeah, squeeze!

Yeah, squeeze tight man! Oh shit man, that is so fucking good on my dick! Oh, I can feel the muscles in your ass when you do that! Yeah – squeeze it again!"

"Hey Jamie, am I the only guy that had you as his first fucker? I mean, have you ever fucked any other guys for their first time?"

"Oh yeah man, oh yeah! I don't know how I get so lucky so often, but there are a lot of male virgin asses out there just waiting for some horny guy like me to strip their pants off of 'em, and tell 'em to spread it – I'm coming in man – open up your ass man – I'm coming in! There are a lot of horny guys, wanting some 'gay guy sex,' that have just never gotten it. Just like you! Be proud man, you are getting a real fucking, a real man-to-man fucking!! Maybe this should be called a 'Man-in-Man' fucking! How's your ass doing, man?"

"Oh shit man. God lying here getting fucked by you and feeling you on me while you are talking about fucking some other guy is so fucking hot to me. Shit man, I'm about to explode just feeling you and listening to you. Jamie, did you get to do any new guy, for his first time, that was really, really special to you? Tell me about your hottest fuck with some new guy's ass."

"Well shit man, I'm in the middle of it right now, but I'm more than willing to tell you about one guy that I just can't get out of my mind. It was about maybe three or four years ago. He was fucking gorgeous! Stood about five foot eleven, had short blond hair, a face you could kiss all day long, and an ass that you could stick your face up in and never come back out from. I remember how I used to blow air up in his ass. Oh God, he loved that!"

"What – you did what?"

"Oh, pull his ass cheeks apart, put my face right up in there right at his asshole, blow air up in his ass and fill his ass with hot man air, right out of my lungs. Hey – I'll show you when I pull my dick back out of your ass. First a dick, then hot air, your ass is getting it tonight!"

"Oh fuck! Oh shit man! Oh Jamie, I'm getting too damned turned on with this. How did you find that guy and what did you do?"

"Found him in a restroom at a theater one night. I was there alone, and, of course, horny as hell like normal, and this guy, his name is Chris, came in while I was at the urinal taking a piss. I, of course, had a hard-on. And I sure as hell was not hiding it from any guy that wanted to see it. He looked, and I let him. We were the only two in there, thank goodness, and for that, I have always been glad, and he was so damned interested in what I was stroking, he missed his aim at the urinal. I looked at him, smiled, and asked, 'Want this?' He almost wilted on the floor. He took a big – very big, deep breath. He looked at me and almost screamed, well not really screamed, but he sure was vocal about it, and he said, 'Oh my God, yes! Yes I do, but man, I've never touched another guy's dick before.' I thought he was about to faint!"

"Shit man – fuck me Jamie – fuck me hard! Ram me man! This is getting me so damn horny even with you up in my ass all the way, I want more! Oh go on – tell me about that pretty Chris guy. What happened?"

"I turned toward him, I was definitely done pissing by then, and I just kind of moved over closer to him, and told him to grab it. He moved real slow. I could definitely tell he had never touched some other guy's dick before. His hand finally reached it. My cock jumped and jerked all by itself as if he had jerked on it. Hell man, I think I almost shot off with him just touching it slightly. He was so damn hot!"

"Hey Jamie, how old was this guy?"

"Oh – he was like twenty five, then. Yeah, he was twenty five. I remember how he told me that he had been thinking about seeing if he could find some guy that he could have sex with, since he was already twenty five, and wanted to see if it was really as hot actually doing it, as what he had kind of dreamed of when he got on the internet and read some of the stuff on there. He was there at the theater with his girlfriend that night, and I told him that doing it in the restroom was not a good idea, but if he'd come to my place right after the movie was over, I'd let him play with me, and since he kept saying, 'I want fucked, I want fucked, will you please fuck me,' I told him that I'd fuck him and make him damn glad that, that was still just a girlfriend, and not a wife yet. Yeah – my telling him that I'd fuck him sounded like I was doing him a favor. Shit man – if you could just see the ass on that guy! I fucked the hell out of that tight ass, I blew air up in that tight ass, I kissed that ass, I bit that ass, I chewed on that ass, I rimmed that tight ass, I stuck my tongue up in that ass, I buried my face in that tight ass. I loved that tight ass! What a virgin ass he brought to me that night! That ass was like having a major dessert, after having a big steak dinner! What an ass that guy has got!"

"Oh shit man! Oh crap! Why in the hell couldn't I have met somebody like you before I was married? Jamie – why didn't you come find me in some restroom before I got married? Jamie, I've fucked a lot before, you know us straight guys, we've always got to prove our manhood by fucking everything, anything, and every night, but man – oh man – no fucking has ever felt this good to me! Oh man, oh Jamie – fuck the hell out of me – fuck me hard, and tell me about you fucking that Chris guy! He did come over to your place, right?"

"Oh yeah, he did. I had given him my address while we were still in the restroom, and I told him that this was finally his chance, that he had better show up. He did! When he got there he told me how he actually just kind of dumped his girlfriend and made some stupid excuse about not feeling good. Well – let me tell you, if he didn't feel well – he sure never got a chance to throw up that night. I gagged him a lot, but with his mouth full of dick, he sure never got a chance to heave if he had actually needed to."

"Hey, he was just making an excuse, right? He wasn't feeling sick was he?"

"No! Hell no! Yeah – he gagged a lot! When you've never had a dick stuck down your throat and you want everything that's sticking out there, right in front of you – well hell – a lot like you did the other night, you are going to gag! He finally learned how to just relax his throat and let the ole pole slide in, but that first night, he was like a five year old kid at Christmas with a present he had wanted his whole life! After he got here, I dropped my gym shorts that I had on, and of course that's all I had on, and I thought he was going to pass out right there. He kept yelling about how big it was! I guess completely naked made it look bigger than it did earlier when I had pants on and it was just sticking out! Hell, his seven or seven and a half wasn't that much smaller. He had a fucking good dick on him! Stiff as a steel re-enforcing rod! That son of a bitch wouldn't bend even if it had an eighteen wheeler drive over it! And I had it up in my ass often enough to be a damn good judge about it. When he got done with my ass a few times, I think I knew how that damn hammer handle had felt to you! God, that guy can really fuck an ass, let me tell you. I guess his not doing it, and yet wanting to do it for so long really, really made him a beast in bed when he finally got the chance!"

"I said he learned how to relax his throat and just let it slide in, well he sure learned how to let his ass relax and let it slide in there too. That first night, he was nervous, nervous as hell, but anxious. I'm sure it was kind of the same feeling as the first time he fucked his girlfriend, only this time it was with a guy, and he knew he was about to get a man's cock up in his ass, and up inside of himself, and he was fucking anxious for that! He kept telling me how he had been wanting this. He told me how he had laid in bed on his gut and spread his legs and made – make-believe, that some guy was on him, in him, and fucking the hell out of his ass. He told me how he pumped his body up and down on the bed as if some guy was ramming his ass and making his body jump up and down while he was pounding his ass and getting fucked. He told me that before he came to my place, he had called his company and left a message that he was not going to be in the next day, once again that he was not feeling well, and told me that if it was possible for him to spend the night, he wanted to be able to, and not have to leave. He said that if he couldn't stay, he'd understand, and then he'd just go home and try to find something around the house to use on his ass that made him feel good. I told him I was more than glad to let him stay the night, and that by the next day his ass was going to be so fucking sore, from just getting fucked, that there was no way in hell that he was going to want to find anything else to put up in there. And believe me – that is exactly the way it turned out! You remember that dildo I used on your ass the other night? You took about ten inches of it. Well Chris took the whole eighteen inches! I started that thing up in his ass, and his ass just ate the whole thing! You know it's a double headed dildo and is really designed for two guys to use it together at the same time. Well, I never got a chance to get my ass on my end of it. Man – that Chris was fucking ready! He was more than ready! He was anxious! I have no idea of what he had been reading on the internet, but whatever it was, it sure as hell was getting him hot and ripe. Fact is, I wonder just how many trips to the restroom he made a night, just praying that he'd find some other horny guy in there that would do him. Well, that night, it worked out, and it worked out for both of us!"

"Oh God Jamie – oh shit man – what a fucking night you had that night! Oh man, did he get fucked right away? Did he just lie down and tell you to get on him and fuck him?"

"Well, yeah kind of – but not really!"

"What do you mean? Jamie, what do you mean kind of, but not really?"

"He saw some of my dildos in a drawer, and they got him all turned on. He told me he had seen some like them advertised on the internet and just the pictures of them got him all turned on, so when they were there, and he could just reach out and touch one, he actually shot some juice without even touching his dick. He told me he really wanted to start with the smallest one and use each one until he got to one that was too big for him to get up in his ass. Mike, what a horny guy for some guy that had never played that way before. I'm serious, I think he wanted the kitchen sink rammed up in that ass of his that night!"

"Oh Jamie you are making me so fucking horny listening to you. How in the hell can a guy get any hornier, than when he's already got the dick of death stuck up in his ass and a hot dude like you lying on top of him, fucking his ass, I do not know, but man I am getting hotter and hotter as you talk. Getting fucked by you and listening to you tell me about you and Chris together has got my whole system ragging! I feel like my heart is pounding in my chest! Oh Jamie, fuck me and let be hear how you fucked that Chris guy! God that is so fucking hot! Man I feel like we are in a three-way here. I love this!"

As Jamie did fuck the hell out of Mike, he realized also that doing the fucking and the thinking back and talking about his friend Chris was a major fucking turn on to him too. For a few moments he kind of replaced Mike, and

Mike's ass, with his old friend Chris, and Chris's ass, and just made believe that he was back in Chris's ass again. That really got him all excited!

"Well, Chris decided that he wanted to see just how much dick, how big of a dick, he could take before he took me. So I told him to lie down on the bed on his gut, and I started in with the smallest one, and worked up the line to the next to the biggest. It's that one lying over there. That one measures right at seven inches around, of course not in diameter, but around the outside, and is fourteen inches long from the tip down to the balls. He took almost that whole damn thing! Seriously, his very first time getting fucked with a dick or a dildo, and he took about twelve inches of a dildo seven inches around. Mike, I was shocked shitless. He had one fucking hungry ass. Hell man, I was proud of him when he took the skinnier ones, the ones more like the thickness of a normal cock, but then after those went up in there so easy, he insisted he wanted to see what that bigger one felt like. Shit man, he took that thing like he did that all the time! The only one he didn't do that night is that really big one. The one the makes you think you are getting fisted when you take it. I measured it around once, and it's actually bigger than when I measured my hand, so now whenever I feel like I want fisted, but don't have anybody around to do me, I sit on it."

"Oh fuck man – oh shit! Oh God Jamie, for a young guy, you sure as hell, have lived doing some good stuff! I saw that damn thing over there and I figured is was supposed to be some kind of a joke or something. You actually put that up inside of your ass!?"

"Yeah – yeah. Yeah I do. I might need to be on the horny side a little, but what the hell, I'm always there anyway."

"O.K., O.K. Quit dreaming about getting that fucking thing up in your ass and start humping me again. You're slowing down back there. Pound my ass and tell me about you finally getting into Chris's butt! You did finally fuck that sweet ass didn't you?"

"Oh hell yes I did. Oh man did I! He got me so fucking turned on by letting me put those dildos up in his ass, once I got in him, I pumped probably only two or three times, and all hell let loose in my dick! I shot his ass so fucking full of cum that it squirted out with me just trying to fuck him some more. That was the first time he had ever felt cum up in his ass, and he was shocked and surprised at how warm it was. Man, did I have a pussy cat in bed with me after that! He was all over me, loving on me, kissing on me, shit man, he finally had the chance to see what the gay sex stuff was, and he ate it up. Oh God Mike, hang on man!! Oh hang on man! I'm just fucking about ready to let you and your ass find out, for your first time, what some hot cum feels like when it gets shot up in your ass. Oh Mike – my dick is so loaded it feels like it's a fucking shotgun just about ready to fire and fucking explode! Oh man, hold on! Oh Mike get ready man, get ready! Oh man, I'm about ready to let you have it! Oh you ready man? Oh Mike!! Oh Mike – – here it cummmes man – – here it cummmmes!!! Oh shit man!! Oh shit!! Oh God! Oh – I just fucking loaded you man! You just took a whole fucking bunch of me! Oh Mike your ass is full of me, man. I just dumped about a quart of cum up in you! Oh man, I am fucking exhausted! Damn your ass is good!"

You Want What?
Chapter Six:
One Hungry Ass

"Oh Jamie, don't pull it out, don't pull it out! Hey man, leave it in me! Fuck me some more, yeah do me some more!"

As Jamie laid exhausted and completely whipped on Mike's back, he raised his head up enough to tell Mike that he was too exhausted to do anymore fucking right then. "Mike, oh shit man, I'm fucking whipped man! Shit man I fucked your ass harder than any ass I've fucked lately. Shit man, for some guy that was screaming just a few days ago that he couldn't take anything up in his ass, you sure have changed your mind. Mike, I've got to rest and re-catch my breath!"

"O.K. man, O.K., but put some fingers or something up in me then! Please! Jamie, I need to feel something up in my butt! I want something up in my butt!"

"O.K., I'll finger you some while I rest, but man, I've got to re-coop some. Your ass wore the hell out of me man! You've got one hot fucking ass! Man, my dick is completely worn out! Man, are you sure you don't get fucked all the time? Man you sure as hell can take it back there like a pro!"

As Jamie pulled out of Mike's ass and repositioned himself beside the hot man and the hot ass that he had just exploded in, he started his fingers on his right hand, kind of, into Mike's ass. He moved them very slowly and very carefully so as to have Mike stay nice and anxious to have his ass played with.

He had completely fucked the hell out of that ass, but if Mike was still anxious to have it played with, he sure did not want Mike to change his mind.

"Come on man, come on. Put some fingers up in me please! Jamie, I want to feel some fingers up in my ass! Please!"

With that statement of encouragement, Jamie decided that doing the fingers in the ass slowly was definitely not the action that Mike was now looking for. Jamie tucked his fingers up close together and with a strong question in his mind about if this was really the right thing to do or not, he rammed all four fingers up and into Mike's ass. One strong shove!

"Oh God yes! Oh God yeah, push!" Mike very loudly exclaimed. "Oh Jamie, push 'em in me man, yeah, push 'em in me!"

Jamie was completely confused at Mike's rather profound insistence, of having Jamie ram his ass with his fingers, but Jamie obeyed the orders and tucked his thumb in close beside his fingers and pushed hard. He questioned if this was really the right thing to be doing to some guy that just now started playing around with his ass, but he had been strongly told that, some strong action back there, was what Mike wanted.

"Oh man – oh God, yes Jamie – yes do that, do that!"

"Mike, I'm about ready to do a complete fisting back here if I push any harder. You want my fist up in there?"

"Yes, yes I think I do! Oh Jamie, the only thing I could think of since I was over here the other day was you playing in my ass. Jamie, I have been so damn anxious to get back over here and do this, I've lost all concentration in doing the normal stuff. I have wanted to get back over here so bad ever since you pushed those dildos up in me the other day! Yeah I want your fist up in me, I guess. I guess, man, yeah I guess I do! Jamie, I'm not sure what I want except that I know I need something up in my ass and right now your hand is feeling really good to me. I've been dreaming about you doing this to me ever since you told me about you getting fisted. Oh man that made me hard and hot! Yeah, yeah I want your fist up in me. Yeah man, yeah – push on it! Yeah, push hard! Yeah, please push on my ass hard! Really hard!"

Jamie put some more lube on his hand and his wrist, and did as he was told so emphatically to do – push his hand up in there! Without hardly any warning at all, his hand did, almost, just fall into Mike's ass. Even with an ass as hungry as Mike's was right then, when Jamie's knuckles popped in, Mike did let out a screaming yell.

"Oh my God man, oh my God! Oh shit man that hurts – oh God man that hurt – oh shit man! Oh Jamie, that cid hurt!"

"Lie still Mike, lie still! Lie still for just a moment and let your ass close around my wrist! Lie still!"

"Oh Jamie, oh shit man – oh fuck! Oh, I should have realized that if your hand went up in me it was going to hurt! Oh shit man, I was just so fucking turned on by the fucking that you gave me, and all of the time I've dreamed about you putting your hand up in there! I just got too fucking excited and too fucking anxious to have something else done to me. Oh shit that hurt when you snapped in! God your knuckles felt like the sides of a railroad car going up in me! Damn man, I should have been smart enough to know getting a hand pushed up in there was going to have to hurt for a second. But man, I was just so damn anxious for it. I guess I really didn't care! I just wanted your hand up in there."

"Mike, I was sure it was going to hurt some if I pushed it on in, but man you just kept begging like you had been fisted before! You O.K.? Is your ass feeling O.K. now?"

"Yeah, it's feeling pretty good now. Yeah, I can sure see now that once a fist gets pushed up in there, a guy's got to just lie here a minute and let the pain pass don't he? Jamie, I never thought about it hurting like that. I was so damn horny for you to do some more hot stuff to me back there that I never thought about what it might feel like once your whole hand goes in. Man, wow! That was unexpected! Oh shit man, how fucking big is my asshole now? Wow, I sure did not expect that!"

"Yeah, I'm not too surprised. When you first asked me to put some fingers up in you I kind of wondered if I should or not, but you were begging so much, I figured, O.K. – he wants it – do it! You doing O.K. now? How's my hand feeling up in there now?"

"Now it's feeling damn good! Real good! Wiggle your fingers some so I can feel them move. Oh yeah – yeah, do that again! Oh Jamie, that feels so fucking good! Hey man, now I'm glad I kind of made you do it. Got to admit that if I had realized that sharp of a pain would hit when your hand pops in, I might not have wanted it, but now – hey man – this is living. Yeah, wiggle your fingers! Oh Jamie, this is something I never thought I'd ever get to do or feel. Oh man, now I know why you get fisted! Oh Jamie, oh shit man! This is great!"

"Yeah man, and I do get fisted as often as I can. You told me the other day you wanted to fist me some time, and I think we moved way closer to that now. Once a guy is fisted, then he knows what it's like on the receiving end, and then he can do the fisting. Mike I've got to tell you that you simply shocked the hell out of me over and over. After you first yelled at me that you can't get fucked, I figured that if I just got to suck on you, I'd be doing good, and now all of a sudden, here we are, lying side by side each other, and I've got my hand up in your ass! Damn man, you are one prize piece! You have gone from virgin boy to full action sex guy in just fucking moments. Mike, most guys that finally get fisted don't get it until after they've thought about it and kind of talked it over with other guys for a long time. You are the first guy that I know of that got it so fucking fast and so soon. Man, I can tell you've really been wanting to do this stuff for a long time, but you just never went out and found it, did you?"

"You know Jamie, I know damn well that internally, I've wanted action like this for years, and just refused to admit it. I mean after all man, any guy that tries to fuck his own ass with a hammer handle, he must be open game for this type of stuff, don't you think?"

"Hey Mike, I know of a guy that fucked himself with a baseball bat once before he started playing around with guys! He told me that once he got that bat up in his ass, he knew he needed to start finding some real dick to use back there."

"Oh fuck shit man, which end? Did he use the smaller end or the big end? Oh God, a baseball bat up in his ass? Ouch, damn man, he sure should have felt that!"

"Well, I asked him the same question when I found out about it. He
told me that he used the smaller end first, but then getting more and more
anxious for more fun, he finally turned the bat over one day, put the smaller end
on the floor, and sat down on the big end. He said he did not, of course, get as
much of the bigger end up in his ass as he did the smaller end, but he admitted
that it felt better. He said forcing his ass open, enough to get the thick end of
it in, was a major turn on."

"Oh shit man, I can't believe that! Wow, what a fucking turn on that
is. Hey – Jamie – did you ever do that?"

"Hell yes! Man, after hearing him tell about putting that bat up in his
ass, I had to try it! He was right, felt damn good, too! Never told my brother
of just why I wanted to borrow his baseball bat for the weekend though. I just
told him that I and some other guys were wanting to do some batting practice
at the city park that week-end. I did make sure I got all of the grease off of it
first though, before I gave it back to him."

As Mike laid there enjoying the feelings of having Jamie's hand
firmly stuck up in his ass, and also listening to Jamie talk about his friend that
had used a baseball bat on his ass, and Jamie's own personal use of a bat, he
said, "Oh Jamie, push in father! Can you put your hand up in me farther? Oh
man, this is feeling good!"

"Are you sure? You sure you want me to do that?"

"Yeah! Yeah I do. I'm so fucking hot just knowing that you are up
inside of me, and listening to you tell about that guy that fucked himself with a
baseball bat, and you fucking yourself with a bat, you've got me all turned on
and hot! Jamie, yeah, please go up in me as far as I can take it, O.K.? Please?
I want to feel your hand way up in me!"

"Yeah Mike, I will, if you want! Yeah, let me get in position here and
let's see how far up in you I can go! Now if it gets uncomfortable, you let me
know, O.K.?"

"Oh man, the way I feel right now, you could probably push it up in
me and make it come out of my mouth and it wouldn't feel uncomfortable.

Jamie, this is so fucking good! Man, I knew I was needing some treatment like this, but man I had no idea of how bad I wanted it. Jamie, I am so damn glad you told me the other day you wanted to suck on me. Shit man – that had to take guts to tell me that, but man, there had to be some kind of an unexplained connection between you and me to make you do that. Oh Jamie, ram my ass! Let me feel your hand up in there as far as you can go! Reach up in me man!"

Jamie did as Mike was begging for, and for more than fifteen or twenty minutes he continued his fisting adventures up into Mike's interior and during the entire time, he continued to hear Mike begging for, "More, yeah deeper man, do me more!"

Finally after the fifteen or twenty minutes of getting fisted and begging for Jamie to put it in farther – farther, Mike finally told Jamie that he thought maybe he had finally hit his limit.

"How far up in me are you? How far did you get in? I can feel your hand up in there, but how far is it?"

"Well, we'll measure it after I pull out, but from the looks of my arm, the part I can still see, I think I got my hand, my wrist and about seven or eight inches of my arm up in you. Still feeling good?"

"Oh God yes it does! You mean, you've got about seven or eight inches more than your wrist up in me? Is that what you mean?"

"Yeah, that's what I'm saying. I will say one major thing for you, and that is – you love to get fisted! You have got one hungry ass man, one hungry ass! Mike, I can sure understand now why you tried to fuck yourself with that hammer handle once. You were real ass hungry back then, and when using that handle on yourself didn't work out so well, then you just got all afraid that anything back there would feel the same way. The way you took my hand and arm up in you today, I'm really surprised that you never tried doing something else back there since that hammer day. Really man, I'm shocked that the way you went for this today, that you've never tried something else. You've never tried anything else, right?"

As Mike laid there encouraging Jamie to keep moving his hand and arm around so that he could have the good inner feelings that he was now enjoying up inside, he attempted to answer Jamie's question about trying anything else.

"No, I never did. Yeah, I will admit that I sure did want to a few times, and I've really dreamed about trying something again, but it just never happened."

"What ideas did you have? What other things did you think about trying?"

"Oh some of them were probably pretty stupid, and I'm probably glad I never did them, but one in particular that I can really remember was really looking at the trailer-hitch ball, on the back of a friend's truck one day."

"The trailer hitch ball!? Talk to me man, talk to me! This sound interesting!"

"I didn't do it Jamie, I didn't do it. Oh how I wanted to, but I never did!"

"Wait a minute here, wait a minute! You didn't do what? What was your idea about the trailer hitch ball?"

"Oh, I and a friend by the name of Tony were out at the lake one day fishing, and we were using his truck. When we were getting our gear out of the back of the truck, I noticed the steel trailer-hitch ball sticking out on the back of the bumper, and all of a sudden I had this, kind of a rush, wishing I could just strip off all of my clothes, and sit my ass down on that shinny steel ball, and let it go up in my ass. All of a sudden, I wanted that ball up in me. Oh man, just the idea of that ball of steel up in my ass was such a fucking turn on! I really wanted to feel that up inside of me, but I didn't do it! I wanted to, but I didn't do it!"

"Uh, did that Tony guy know what you were thinking? Did he have any reason to know what you wanted to do?"

"No, no. Hell man, I couldn't tell some other guy that all of a sudden I wanted his trailer-hitch ball up in my ass! It looked exciting, but I had to just let it go. I do admit though, that during that whole day, I kind of kept thinking about it, and I kept wishing I could try it! I made stupid excuses more than once to go get something out of the back of the truck, just so I could look at that steel ball sticking out from that bumper, and how I wanted to just strip my Levi's off, and sit down on it and let it fill my ass. Oh, just the idea of that mass of steel up in my butt – that turned me on!"

"Well – hey – if Tony had not been there, think you might have done it? If you had been by yourself, think you would have set down on it?"

"Yeah – hell yes I would have! I figured I had tried the hammer handle once, so why not the trailer-hitch. I thought maybe it would be better than the hammer was. Well anyway, I was hoping it would be. I will admit that a couple of times I wished I was out there all by myself and could do that. I even wondered a few times if there was anyway I could make an excuse to borrow Tony's truck for some reason, and then take it out some place, real private, and sit on it. Jamie, I'm being real honest with you about some of my wild ideas, but then I figure, hell man – the guy has his arm stuck up in my ass, so what in the hell do I need to be primp and proper about. You had the guts to tell me you wanted to suck me off, so I sure as hell can have the guts to tell you that I've wanted to be fucked by some steel ball. I'm really having some serious fun being able to tell you this shit. I guess I've wanted somebody like you around me for a hell of a long time now, and it's finally happening. Jamie, I'm liking this! I thought I was about ready to have you take your hand back out, but after thinking about that trailer hitch ball and how I wish I could have done that, my ass is begging for more! Push your hand up in me again. Push hard, yeah – let me feel your fingers moving around up in my guts! Oh God man! Your hand has got to feel one hell of a lot better than that trailer-hitch ball would have felt! It would have felt good, and I know just the idea of that ball of steel going up in my ass is a fucking turn on, but it sure could not have gone up in me like your hand is doing! Push man, push! Make me think you've got that ball of steel in your hand and you're ramming my ass and my guts with it. Oh man, I can't believe this! I'm finally getting something big up in my ass! Fist me man, fist me! Oh yeah, make a fist, make a fist. I can feel you making a fist up in my ass. Jamie, you folded your hand up into a fist didn't you? Oh yeah man, I can feel it! Oh shit it feels good! Jamie, I can tell this is only the beginning of one long term friendship."

"You know what Mike? Right now I am imagining one year from now. The way you are playing, and the way you want to be playing, I just know that in about a year, we are gonna be looking back and laughing about a lot of stuff. Like the first time you took the big end of a baseball bat – the first time you took that great big dildo – that I still have to put on the floor and squat onto, to get it up in my ass – the first time you got double fisted – and to top it all off, I've got a co-worker that has got a pickup truck with a bright chrome steel trailer-hitch ball on the back of it. I've still got a 'number three,' pool ball – that was put up in my ass in a pool hall one night – but I had never thought of taking a trailer-hitch ball up in my ass. But I sure do like the idea of it! We are gonna borrow his truck someday, and both of us are gonna use that trailer hitch on ourselves – up in our asses! God – just the idea of squatting down on that thing and letting it go up in my ass, is really turning me on. That would be something new for me. Something that I had never thought of before. Imagine, squatting on that ball, bouncing up and down, and making the truck bounce up and down with you! That's almost like getting fucked by a truck!"

"Jamie, I have no idea of what special sniffing powers you must have, but right now I truly do think that when you started following me and then finally telling me you wanted to suck on my dick, you could smell something about me, that really attracted me to you – like some wild horny animal out in the middle of a jungle, finding himself a mate. That truck – how soon can we borrow that truck!? We really need – to borrow that truck!"

Room For Rent
Chapter One:
1265 East Maple

"1265 East Maple – there it is," Jim said to himself.

It was a bright and warm Sunday morning about 10 AM and Jim was using the newspaper ads as a guide, to possibly find himself a good 'in town room' that he could rent to use during the workweek, since he was now going to be working a construction job just a little too far away from home to be able to drive back and forth each day.

Jim worked construction framing and simply had to go to whichever town had the work available. He was a married man, and a daddy of two children, a boy aged three and a girl aged five. He, aged twenty-eight and his wife Barbara, two years younger, certainly did not like the idea of Jim needing to be away from home during the entire week, but they had decided that if they wanted the income, and on a steady basis, that simply was the way life was going to have to be until Jim could get the financing together to start his own small construction company.

The project that Jim was hired onto was a major apartment complex and was going to be a good steady job for at least a year, and that was something that did not happen very often, so the necessity of staying in the city during the week and then going home during the weekend was just going to be a necessity.

Jim had gotten confirmation on Friday afternoon that he was definitely hired and he had called Barbara that afternoon and told her the good news and that he was going to stay in town that weekend to see if he could find a room to rent someplace, and get that little problem off of his mind.

The entire Saturday had come and gone, and he had chased down about twenty different 'room for rent' locations, and nothing, absolutely nothing was turning out to be even slightly acceptable. Dirt, rats, highway traffic, railroad noise, police sirens, you name it, each one had its terrible distractions to being a good place to be, let alone sleep. He easily understood why they were each available, and probably had been for quite some time.

After a very disappointing day Saturday, Jim decided that he just needed to look in some of the less seedy parts of town, and just see if he could locate something that was in his price range, although it would probably have to be a little smaller than what he had been hoping to find.

"1265 East Maple, there it is," Jim again uttered as he pulled his truck up along the curb on the other side of the street.

"Damn, looks pretty nice, especially compared to yesterday's crap!" Jim told himself as he questioned the feasibility of this being a location that would be very happy renting to a construction worker, rather than to maybe some computer guy or maybe a CPA type of guy. He rechecked the newspaper ad:

Room for rent for a gentleman

Large bedroom/shared bath with male owner

Kitchen privileges/covered parking/local phone use

Available by the week or the month/discount for longer term

Rent rate to be discussed upon inspection

1265 East Maple

"Yeah, that's it!" Once again Jim told himself. "Sure does look like something a lot more than my aim of $400 a month to me though. Wonder what the monthly is on this?"

Deciding, that at least looking at it, and then deciding if it was a go or not was the prudent thing to do, since he had taken the time to find it. He had some serious doubts though. Sharp looking place, and in this neighborhood, and anything close to $400 a month sure did not seem to be a possibility, especially when compared to the trash he had looked at the day before. It was total crap, and it too was going for $400 and sometimes $500 a month, and even then some of them were without utilities included.

Jim figured that if it was going to be advertised in the newspaper, then the owner had better expect people to stop by to see what it was and to find out what the dollar figure was going to be since it was not listed in the ad.

After parking his pickup a little more properly, Jim swung his six foot two, two hundred and five pound structure out of the truck and slowly approached the front door, admiring all of the detailed work that had been put into the landscaping of the yard.

With the newspaper in hand, he rang the front doorbell. He waited. He rang the doorbell again. He waited, some more! He turned and saw an SUV parked in the carport and wondered if nobody was home, even though the SUV was parked there, and their ad had hit the newspaper that morning. He rang the doorbell the third time.

From what sounded like from a distance in the house he heard a man's voice yell out, "I'm coming, I'll be right there!"

Jim patiently waited by the door, until he heard it being unlocked and then opened.

As the door swung open, Jim was greeted by a young man, probably about age thirty-three, that had much the same body structure and appearance as Jim did. Only major difference was, the house owner only had a bath towel wrapped around himself, whereas Jim was fully clothed.

Opening the door and at the same time making sure the towel was securely placed, the house owner asked, "Yes, what can I do for you?"

Jim rather held up the paper and said, "I'm here about your ad for a room to rent."

Acting rather confused, the man inside the door, looked at the newspaper, then looked at Jim and asked, "The ad? Is the ad in today's newspaper?"

Jim then, rather kind of confused like, then replied, "Well yeah! Is this 1265 East Maple?"

The, now very confused homeowner then quickly replied, "Yeah – yes it is! I'm sorry – I did not know they got my ad in today! I'm sorry. Hey, here, come on in. I'm sorry, I did not think it was going to be in until tomorrow."

Jim watched the 'rather undressed' man reach forward and unlock the screen door, and pushed it open and again said, "I'm sorry, come on in! Really I did not know they got my ad in today's paper."

The homeowner held the screen door open with his right hand, and continued to maintain total control of the damp bath towel with his left hand. "Please come in! I'm sorry, I did not expect anybody today. Forgive me, I was taking a shower when I heard the doorbell. I assumed that it was some friend of mine or I would have yelled that I needed to get dressed. I'm sorry, I'm feeling all confused here. See, I know the people in the ad department of the newspaper, and they told me that they did not think they could get my ad in till tomorrow, so I did not know it was already in there. Oh, I'm Todd!"

Reaching out to grasp the extended hand for a hand shake, Jim replied, "Hi, I'm Jim. Sorry, I kind of caught you at a bad time."

"Hey man! Not your fault at all!" Todd replied as he let the screen door close, and he then closed the main door.

As he re-tucked the top of his bath towel in, to make sure it was secure, Todd then added, "Well Jim, I sure am kind of embarrassed about the way we have met, but since you might be interested in the room, and since I don't always wear a three piece suit in the house, I kind of guess the idea of you seeing me almost totally naked is a pretty good way of getting to meet each other, since I'm sure this will happen a number of times if you and I live together."

Jim jokingly laughed and without even letting on a hint that he truly was quite overtaken with the 'almost totally naked body' that was standing in front of him, he simply said, "Hey no big deal. I've taken a lot of gang showers with the guys when back in high school days, so it's no big deal. You want me to wait here while you get dressed, or something?"

"No actually no, if it's O.K. with you. You've already seen almost the 'all of me,' so why in the hell try to act all primp and proper now? You're a guy, I'm a guy and, hey – big deal."

Accepting that Todd was comfortable with just keeping the towel on, Jim felt slightly uncomfortable in that every time he looked at Todd, he felt like he was slightly admiring his physic, and that was making Jim just a little uncomfortable. He did not expect to be interviewed by an almost naked man, and the sharp structure that Todd was displaying was just a little too close to the well defined structure, that he personally had strived for during all of his long hours, pushing tons of weight, in the weight room.

Todd led the way down the hall. to the bedroom in question.

"Damn man, this is nice!" Jim expounded. "Man, this is a nice sized room!"

Todd rather shook his head, and quietly replied, "Yeah, yeah it is."

Jim managed an, "Uh – O.K. Your ad, it doesn't give a dollar figure, and now that I'm here in your neighborhood, and after seeing this room too, I'm kind of figuring that I might be looking way above my head – dollar wise."

Todd did not immediately give a dollar figure, but rather told Jim that there was no, set-in-concrete firm figure, and he was wanting to know for about how long Jim might want the room and where he was working and quite a number of other items.

Jim gave Todd a very complete detailed commentary on his working situation, his family situation and his need for a room for just the work week.

As they stood there slightly discussing Jim's situation, Todd was becoming more and more convinced that if it meant paying HIM – Jim – the money to stay there, he was about willing to do it, just to have that hunk of a man around.

Todd was noticing how damned hunky this young daddy guy was, even though he was fully dressed and not showing all of the bare skin that he himself was displaying. Looking through the cloth, so to say, Todd liked what he could imagine was being hidden underneath!

After a rather extensive conversation, some material that was kind of necessary, and some material that was simply letting Todd get to know Jim better, and Jim's attitudes on life a little better, Todd said, "Jim, I've never rented this room to anybody before, since I'm O.K. financially and really don't need the income, but I decided that having someone else around some of the time would be good, and that's the only reason I decided to do it. Friends have told me that I should charge at least $500 or $600 a month since the whole house is available, but I'm going to be damn honest with you and tell you that money is not my main aim. You and your family are trying to make it financially, and you are only going to be here during the work week, and just having you around part of the time is part of the pay off to me. Jim, I'm going to be real honest with you and let you know everything so you can make the decision. I think I've pretty well read you as being a pretty open minded kind of guy. You seem to have some pretty good attitudes about stuff in general. If I told you that I am a gay guy, and there will probably be some of my friends around some of the time – and sometimes for overnight – if you can accept that, I'm willing to rent you this room for $200 a month. Jim, if I can have some guy like you using this room, and you said you will need it for at least a good year, then to me, part of my pay back is just having some good guy around that I can talk to part of the time, or maybe fix supper for if our schedules hit just right. What do you say? Sound like a deal to you?"

"Jim, I'm not gay. I'm married and a daddy of two kids. I sure don't have anything against gays, but are you thinking that if you rent me this room, that I'm expected to join in on your gay stuff?"

"No Jim, NO! No, I sure did not mean to imply that at all. I just wanted you to know the real stuff before you decide if this will work for you. If I have some guy in for the night, and he is still here the next morning, I need to know that you understand and that doesn't freak you out any. If you want the room, it is strictly total business between you and me, and my buddies too. They will know you are a straight guy! And what you pay for rent is none of their damn business. Seriously Jim, I'm hoping you will take it. I do want you to understand though that we will be sharing a bathroom, and I do not intend to, nor do I ever, put pants on just to go from my bedroom to the bathroom. If you know that seeing me running around the house without any pants on is a problem, then maybe this will not work. As far as I'm concerned, if you run around naked, that sure is not going to bother me, but that is up to you. You're a grown man, and I'm a grown man and I really don't think seeing each other naked once in awhile should be a problem, but like I said, it's up to you."

"I will admit," Todd continued, "seeing each of us naked will be a hell of a bigger problem for me than for you, I know. You are no slob and I will just have to make a very firm promise to you that I will respect you and not make you uncomfortable with any funny actions or comments. I hope you can trust me that I will not try anything with you. I may tell you once in awhile that I'd like to or tell you that I wish I could, but that will just be talk. I think you probably have been around other gays before and you probably already know how we can be pretty direct in saying what we'd like to do and with whom."

"When I thought about maybe renting this room out just to have somebody around once in awhile, I never had any imagination that somebody like you might be the person. I'm willing to make it real cheap for you, so that you can save toward that business you want, and just having some guy like you around would be a big pay off to me. I think you and I could get along real well, and I'd sure rather give you a deal and have you around here than to charge some old fart a lot, and then wish he'd move out! What do you say? You're safe man. I won't let any of my guys get to you! Fact is we just might hang a big sign on your door that states something like, 'Stay out – I'm straight!' "

"Todd, I never imagined that I might get confronted with something like this. All I was doing was trying to find a good room someplace, to rent for the weekdays. I never imagined that I'd run into a situation when maybe I was going to have to decide if what goes on there was acceptable to me or not. Hell man, I would have thought all those dumps I saw yesterday would have been more of the place for something like this to happen, not someplace around here. God Todd! I've got to admit, being able to have a room for only $200 a month could make a guy put up with a lot of stuff that might be a problem for him. But shit man, I'm a married man with a wife and two kids back home. What if somebody found out where I was living during the week?"

"Jim, I was really hoping that being straight forward and honest with you could and would pay off for me, but if knowing that you would be staying with a gay guy, and sometimes, him having some of his men in, overnight, is a problem, then I can understand your position."

"Oh Todd, what a damn decision!" Jim said. "O.K. – now I've got one question for you! Are you a top, or a bottom?"

Room For Rent
Chapter Two:
Mat and Randy

"What!? What in the hell did you just ask me!?" Todd exclaimed more excitedly than any question he had asked in a lifetime. "What in the hell did you just ask? Am I a top or a bottom!? Jim, what in the hell are you asking?"

"Hey Todd, I've been around enough to know that gays are usually either a top, doing the fucking, or a bottom, the one getting it in the ass. Right? Well – am I right?"

"Yeah Jim, you are right, but it's not quite that cut and dried. It's not always just the one way. Some guys do both. Jim, have you played around? Have you done some gay stuff before?"

"Hey Todd, I'd rather not come across as some guy that does everything, but yeah, I will admit that a couple of times I kind of did the guy thing. If you have your friends over here and I am renting this room, I'm not going to be all shocked out of my wits with what happens. I've watched some other guys do some stuff that I've never done, but at least it's not like I think nobody, ever does that stuff. I kind of know some of the stuff that goes on."

"God Jim, you've got me all shocked here. You're married! Right? You've got kids! Right?"

"Yeah and yeah Todd, but like you already said, its not always just the one way. Yeah, I do admit that since I've been married, I've not done any of the guy stuff, but that does not mean that I think all of the guys have stopped doing it."

"Jim, when – uh – what did you do?" Todd so anxiously asked in his state of shock.

"Oh hell, it was years ago when I was in construction school. Nothing big, but none the less, enough for me to learn what happens behind some closed doors, or maybe like one of my experiences, out in the dark back alley."

"Out in the back alley?" Todd excitedly asked. "What in the hell happened in a back alley? Jim, tell me about it? Can you tell me? I'd like to hear it if you can tell me. Can you tell me?"

"Yeah, I guess so. It was all kind of a set up by a couple of guys that I did know in high school. They set it up so that they could – well – what should I call it – they could do me. Use me."

"Jim, what do you mean – do you? What do you mean by that?"

"They fucked my ass!"

"Jim, please tell me, what happened. This was in a back alley? This was while you were still in high school? Jim, please, can you tell me what happened?"

"God Todd, I feel kind of funny telling you about this. No, this was just after high school. I was in a construction school in Clarkensville, and those guys were attending a Junior College there, and they knew I was in town too. I've never told anybody what happened that night. Even after the cops left I never told anybody. Todd, this is something that I have lived with for like eight years. I've had to hide what happened and I've never told anybody."

"Jim, from the way you are acting, maybe now is the time to finally get it off of your chest. Maybe you would feel better if you actually told somebody what happened to you. What do you think? Hey man, look at it this way! Tell me about it, get it off of your chest and nobody but you and I will know you talked about it. O.K.? Can you do that?"

"Maybe so Todd, maybe so! I've hidden that night from me and everybody else for so damn long, maybe I will feel better if I do tell somebody, just somebody about it."

Jim kind of stood there and got very mellow, and Todd stood beside him quietly encouraging him to share his experience, if he wanted to and thought it would be good to do so.

"Todd, it was the first year after high school. I was working in a pizza shop in that town, at night. It was real late at night and like usual, after we closed, I stayed and cleaned up the place and took all the trash out and did that kind of stuff. We had closed up shop and the guy I worked with had left and I was there all alone. I went out the back door to take the trash out and these guys attached me in the alley. One of them grabbed me, and the other one turned the button on the inside of the door and slammed it shut. That locked the door closed. Our shop was in the very middle of a very long row of stores in a shopping center. So to get back in the shop, if the back was locked and there was nobody inside to let you in, you had to walk all of the way around about fifteen or twenty stores to just get back to the front. Well anyway, after they locked us out, they told me that they had looked at my ass while we were in high school together, in the locker and shower room, and they decided that they wanted it. They told me that some guy by the name of Sammy, whoever in the hell that was supposed to be, had told them that he had fucked me once, and they said it was now their turn. I had never been fucked, and that Sammy guy – I guess they were just making him up. Anyway, yeah I did know both of the guys. They had always been a hell of a lot of trouble in school, and one of them, Mat, his father was on the school board, so nobody ever did anything about them. The teachers just let it all ride. Anyway, always doing whatever they wanted and getting away with it, and since we were now in a different town, they had decided they wanted to fuck my ass. And they did! Once again, just doing what they wanted to do, regardless of what somebody else thinks. But this time, they had to really set up a plan to get to me. They knew where and when I was working, so they did the dark back alley thing to me. In the dark alley, they stripped me, and while one held me down the other one fucked me. Then they switched and the other one fucked me. Thank God, they had done that, either to each other enough, or to other guys, that they knew they'd need some KY jelly. That part I was damn thankful for!"

"Jim, were you all alone in that alley? Nobody else around that you could yell to?"

"No, I sure was all alone, well except for big Mat, and his fucking hung buddy Randy! God he was hung, and especially when he's aiming it toward a guy that has never had a dick up in his ass before. Anyway, yeah – there was nobody even close to earshot that I could have yelled to. They damn well knew that too. That's why they got me in the alley and not in the pizza shop. I think they knew that to attach me in the shop could have been real bad for them if they were found in there, so anyway, they used the alley. I think maybe they were afraid that if they were in the inside, something could be seen through the front windows, especially since the place was pretty open, and not too many walls."

"Once they both got a hold of me and told me what was going to happen, then they stripped me down all the way. I was totally naked. Bare ass and all. Mat actually threw me down on my gut and then Randy held me down while Mat rammed my ass. That was the first time I had ever been fucked, and it hurt! I tried to yell, but Randy kept me from yelling. After about ten minutes in my ass, it did kind of start feeling better, but I never let them know that. I knew Mat was only the first one, and I had seen Randy's rod in the school shower room before, and it was a fucking monster. The whole time Mat was fucking me I was scared to death about knowing that Randy was going to be pushing that damn big thing of his, up in my ass. Well, it finally happened! They switched places and Randy rammed me like he was fucking a hog or something. Damn he went in fast and far! And I knew it! Shit man, I really got fucked hard. I thought my insides were all torn up. I thought Mat made me feel full, but once Randy got in me, then I knew damn well, I had taken as much as I could get in me. He fucked me for probably a good ten minutes and then all of a sudden I knew he was, 'giving me a kid,' as he called it. He started yelling, 'Here comes the kid – here comes the kid!' Then he let out a big groan and really pushed his dick up in me and laid on me real hard and heavy. I could feel my ass getting full, but the way it felt I really wasn't sure if it was all cum or some blood with it. From the way it felt, when he first slammed in me, I really did think I was bleeding."

"Oh God Jim, were you O.K.? Were you O.K.?"

"Yeah Todd, I decided later that I was O.K., but I sure didn't think so right away. As soon as Randy got done with of me, they both wiped their drippy dicks on my bare skin, pulled their pants up, jumped into their car and sped off. I stood there all naked, with cum on me, and dripping out of me. I had cum loads from both of those guys up in my ass right then. Hell, after that, I felt like I was pregnant! And I will tell you, right then I sure as hell was damn glad a guy can't get knocked-up by getting fucked in the ass, or after what I went through that night, I probably would have had a litter of kids."

"Oh God Jim, What in the hell did you do? What in the hell did you do then?" Todd anxiously asked with total concern in his voice.

"Well, I got some paper out of the trash can and wiped the cum off of me, and I kept checking my ass with the paper to see if I was bleeding back there or not. I must have checked that five times. I got dressed and started the long walk around to the front of the shop. I knew that once I got there that I could get in, since I did have a front door key. I had a front door key, but nobody had a back door key. That door wasn't supposed to be locked if you were out back. Anyway, I walked. I even felt like I was walking funny. Kind of like I couldn't get my ass put back together completely. I felt like my asshole was still wide open and pushing my ass cheeks apart. I was a mess. I know I must have looked like a mess. My shirt was out, and hell, my pants were probably on wrong side out. Just as I was about four stores away from the pizza shop, a cop car drove up and asked me what I was doing. I had to lie and tell them that I had accidentally locked myself out of the back door, and I was walking around to get back in. I had to prove to 'em that I had a key, and then after we got inside I had to show 'em my time card, with my name on it, to prove that I really did work there. I didn't tell them about me getting fucked in the alley. I knew that if I did, then I'd have problems with Mat and Randy, and I decided – what the hell – I've already been fucked, and I can't undo that, and besides, I also did realize that the longer they were up in me, the better it started to feel, so I thought, well – hell – if I was not all scared, then I might want to try that again some day, and if I tell on them, I know damn well I will never get fucked by either one of them. And, I didn't know of any other guys that I could ask to fuck my ass. So I just kept my mouth shut. I was mad, but I guess my ass was trying to tell me to keep my mouth shut! As I look back, it's real weird. I was forced to get fucked, for my first time, by two guys that made me do it – out in a dark alley – it hurt – and I was scared to death. I thought I had been ripped open inside, and yet I had these stupid feelings that maybe I would want to do this again sometime. I should have been feeling like never – NEVER will I ever allow any guy back up inside of my butt again. Todd, I never felt that way! My whole body had been completely used by those two guys, and I wasn't raging mad! I should have been really, really pissed and mad!"

"Well Jim, did you ever go for it again? Did you ever let either one of them fuck you again?"

"Oh yeah! About a month later, I went to the college dorm where they were students, and in a hallway, I told them that if they made any trouble, I was going to the police department and report what had happened in the alley. From that time on, I went to their dorm room and got it up in the ass, whenever I wanted. I had to admit to them that after that alley situation happened, I kinda decided that I wanted to try it again, but in a better place. Cause it was always in their dorm room, I was trying to make it real rough on them, and at the same time, have some fun in my ass. I'd give the orders, and they acted. I'd show up right before they were supposed to be in class, or just as they were leaving for the dining hall for supper. But they knew what they had to do! I found out eventually that I really did prefer Randy's dick in me the best. That kind of pissed Mat off some, so I'd make him suck me off, which was something that he really did not want to do. He liked to fuck, but not suck. I just told him that because of the cops talking to me that night, and how they kept asking me what had happened to me, I could get backup to support my story about the alley, and they had better do what I wanted. They did! I got fucked about every three or four days by either one of them, or both of them. And Mat, well he's got more than just one of 'my kids' down in his throat."

"Man alive Jim, what an experience! You have never told anybody else about that night or how you then made those guys fuck you whenever you wanted?"

"No, not until right now! Todd, you are really the very first person that I have ever been around that I felt comfortable enough with, to tell it to. Got to remember, I'm really a straight guy, and now I'm married and have kids, so it sure is not something to talk about. But you know, like you said, now that I've said it, I do feel like a big load is off of my back. Keeping total secrets is rough. Thanks for encouraging me to spill that. Yeah, I feel better! I have no idea now where Mat or Randy are, but I do bet that they still wonder if I could come back into their lives and start something about that alley thing. You know Todd, I've been fucked by those guys since then, and it was when I wanted it, but you know, that night in the alley I was plain scared and mad. I'd never been fucked before, and that night, I was not happy! I guess maybe that night was really introducing me to something that I did not know I wanted. You know, I've wondered about that Randy, ever since then. Now I've got to admit that one, maybe, could be used again. He was hot and hung. Well, I'm sure he's still well hung, but I mean when he was just out of high school he had one hell of a well built body. The night this all happened, I could have cared less what he looked like or how he was built, but you know, later, when I was the one deciding that he was going to be fucking my ass, I started to kind of get turned on with how Randy was built. I thought, well hell, if I'm going to have some guy up in my ass, he might as well be some hunky good looking guy that all the girls want to get fucked by, too. I kind of felt like I was getting some of the really good stuff."

"Jim you mentioned earlier that you had done some goofing around after high school, right, and also while at a construction school. Right?"

"Oh yeah. After that one year in that one construction school, it was only a part time thing, I left town and entered a bigger and better school that taught more skills. Yeah, well, it's not quite the same type of story as the alley thing is. At that construction school, I had a roommate and he drank a lot. He's be out for the night, and come back to the room completely plastered, and I guess maybe he had some true gay tendencies, since when he'd come home all plastered, he'd start lying across me, and then start calling me his little doggie and how he loved his little doggie and eventually, he'd end up fucking my ass. After the Mat and Randy thing, yeah, I do admit that I decided that getting it up in the ass was pretty good, so since Bob was drunk and never, 'supposedly,' remembered anything the next day, whenever he tried to get to me, I'd just let him do it. I'd been fucked before, and I decided, no harm done, go for it again. If I really did not want to do it on a particular night, then I'd just push him off and he'd usually lie on the floor for awhile before he woke up enough to get up and go to bed. I guess it all depended on what kind of a mood I was in. A couple of times he fell asleep on top of me, well – I should say, kinda in me, and we slept that way for probably an hour or so, until one of us moved enough to kind of separate. The next day, he'd always ask me what time did he get home and when did he go to bed. He could never remember what he did the night before. He'd keep asking me if he brought some gal home with him. I'd just tell him, 'No. You came home by yourself.' I've got to admit that after he asked that question a couple of times, I wondered if maybe he just kind of, remembered fucking me and he was trying to figure out if he fucked some gal that night, was he just imagining things, or was he trying to make me think he did not know that he was fucking me whenever he got home. I just never told him what really happened. I've always wondered if when he was actually fucking my ass, while he was drunk, did he think he was fucking some gal? Was he really so drunk that he could not tell the difference between fucking a man and a woman? Hell man, he was always so far out of it, he could have thought he was fucking some gorilla. Well, I was enjoying it, I was actually having fun letting some guy fuck my ass that supposedly never realized what he was doing, and I was kind of afraid that if I told him, he'd deny it, and also quit doing it, or move into some other room. I was liking the fuckings that I was getting, whenever I decided, I wanted it. And with his drinking problem, I could have been fucked every night if I wanted."

        "Well Jim, how often did you let him fuck you? How long did this go on?"

"Went on for almost the whole ten months that I was there. Started the week right after we moved in together. He and I went out for a drink at the local bar, but I left before he did. I went back to the room to do some reading, and he showed up later. Much later! He was so drunk I was surprised that he could find the room. He came in and flopped himself down on the little settee that was in our living area. I was sitting there reading one of the school books. He fell over against me, and started calling me 'Little Rover' and kept pawing at me like I was a dog. Well, that night I sure didn't know what in the hell was going on, but I just played along some, so that I didn't sound mad. Anyway he did start playing kind of roughly and kept pawing at me, and finally did slide his hand down inside of the under briefs, which was the only thing that I had on. I immediately wondered if maybe he was gay, but when I tried to ask him, he denied it, but he was so out of it, I'm not sure he even knew who he was playing with, let alone if he was gay or not. I'm not even sure he understood the question. And maybe the answer should have been 'Yes,' and he just did not want to admit it. Maybe he was afraid that I'd leave if he admitted it. Well anyway, it had been quite some time since I had let Mat or Randy play back there, so maybe I did encourage his hand to slide down between the cheeks of my ass. I hadn't been groped back there for way too long, I guess. I know it sounds kind of sick, but I finally asked him if he wanted to fuck his 'Little Rover' puppy and he kind of said yes. When he was kind of lying all over me and putting his hand down in the crack of my butt, he kinda kept calling it my cunt, and then rubbing his hand up and down. I guess I was pretty horny after all of his rubbing on me, all over. I helped him get his clothes off and that was the first time that I had seen his dick. I was shocked! Man, he did not need to act drunk to use that thing on me! I pulled my briefs off and ran into the bathroom and grabbed some Vaseline that was in there and pushed some up in my ass. I know it's not what you are supposed to use, but I figured it was better than letting him and his nine inch dick go up in there all dry. I came back in the living room and I got down on all fours and told him to come and get it. He did! Todd, he was so damn hard and stiff I wondered at that time if he could really be drunk, but seeing that thing and knowing that I was about to get fucked by it, I sure was not going to make him quit acting drunk, if he really wasn't. I wanted that fucking dick up in me! Seriously Todd, and I'm kind of ashamed to admit it, but that night I did feel like I was a bitch dog getting fucked. I was down on all fours on the floor and he was back there pawing around and sniffing and licking my ass, before he finally got his dick in it. If he wasn't really drunk, he sure as hell could play the part! And if he was really drunk, he sure as hell can fuck like a master when he is drunk!"

"God Jim, for straight guy, you sure know how to get your ass fucked, don't you?"

"Yeah, I guess, but it's only been Mat, Randy and that Bob. I haven't done it since I got married."

"Jim, don't you really think this Bob guy really did kind of know what he was doing? Don't you think maybe he was playing a little more drunk than maybe he really was?"

"You know. If he was playing a roll just so he could fuck me, then I was playing a roll too, just to get him to fuck me. After that first night, and knowing the size of that rod, I'd do more than just act like a doggie, just to get him to push that thing up in me."

"Did he ever say anything or do anything that might have made you kind of wonder if he really did remember fucking you?"

"Well, there were only a couple of times that I kind of wondered about some of his comments, but I decided not to ask him, for fear that I might be wrong. One day the instructor was talking about our carpentry tools and how to take care of them. When he was talking about our hammers, Bob was beside me and he started laughing. I looked at him, but he then tried to stifle the giggling that he was doing. Well, when the instructor made a comment about keeping our tools in our tool box and not letting them lie around, Bob kind of like leaned over and just said, 'Yeah, like my hammer!' Then he looked straight at me and kind of winked! I just looked back at him with a very quizzed look on my face, and then he said something like, 'I'll take care of my tool, and do whatever I want with my tool! When I want to use my hammer, I'll use it however I want to use it!' "

"Jim – oh Jim! I really do think Bob was trying to tell you something, don't you?"

"I really don't know! It was all so weird and strange. He just kind of maybe got close to the subject, but I was still too afraid that he really was not meaning that, and I was just putting thoughts in my head. He'd make stupid comments once in awhile, and that time, I really was confused."

"Well, what other stuff did he say that maybe made you think he knew?"

"It was again during a class, when of course we can't talk to each other, just make comments under our breath, and all of us were standing around the instructor in a circle listening and the instructor was talking about getting something tight. Something like nailing a board tight. I swear Bob leaned over and very, and I do mean very softly said something like, 'Yeah, like nailing your tight ass.' I looked at him and asked, 'What!?' He never repeated it. He just laughed but then when we left that class that morning, he did reach over and slap my ass, which was the only time he ever did that, and said something like, 'Come on man, let's go nail it tight!' I looked at him to see what his expression was, but he had turned his head and was looking the other way. I really still do not know if I was reading too much into his comments or not. I pondered that all that day!"

"Well, what happened that night? Did he ever say anything later?"

"No, everything was as normal, and like usual. He did go out drinking again that night, but the way he drank, that really was every night. He came home plastered again. He came in and fell across the coffee table. I helped him get up and helped him get undressed and laid him down in the bed. He kept pawing at me like he did the night he called me 'Little Rover.' He kept telling me to lie down and help him stay in bed. I guess he was afraid that he was going to fall out of bed. So shit man, by this time, with all of his pawing at me, and me getting him all undressed and into bed, I'd gotten kind of ass hungry, since I now had him all undressed and once again saw that dick of his, so I got undressed, grabbed some KY, which, by that time, I knew to always kept on hand, slammed some of it up in my ass and got in his bed beside him.

He kind of acted like he knew I was there, but not really. I decided that if I was going to get fucked by him that night, then I needed to get his dick hard, so I jerked him off a little and it got hard right away. Then out of, I guess desperation, I asked him if he wanted to fuck his 'Little Rover' puppy again. He always seemed to know what you were talking about if you talked about his little doggie. So anyway, I still don't know if he was totally drunk or playing, and at this point, I really did not care, but I got up on my all fours on the bed, and helped him get back behind me. We fucked that way for only about a minute and then I had to lie on my gut to keep him up on top of me and not falling on the floor. He fucks good when he is drunk, unless he was playing more drunk than he really was. He fucked his 'Little Rover' good and strong that night! I had felt like a dog the first time, and I did again that night since I really was the one that made it happen. That night I was actually the aggressor since I do think that if I had not gone for it, and had not gotten him into it, he would have just fallen asleep and slept the rest of the night. Other than the first night, that was the only time that I actually kind of made him fuck me when maybe he had not intended to. I was his puppy doggie again that night! Those were the only two nights when I acted like I was his puppy dog."

"Oh God Jim, I can not imagine you doing that! God man, look at my towel, it's not hanging down very well! You are getting this guy all hot and bothered here – hope you realize it. You do know you are standing here, telling a gay guy all of this stuff. This stuff gets guys like me kinda hot and bothered some."

As Jim looked down at Todd's tented towel, he grinned broadly, looked up at Todd, reached up, pinched his left nipple and asked, "Hey, maybe I should play like I'm 'Little Rover' today – huh!?"

Room For Rent
Chapter Three:
God Man – You Doing Okay?

"Oh my God Jim, what are you saying?"

"Hey Todd, what I am saying is that tent that you are showing down there is making me remember some pretty good feelings from my prior days. Until talking to you, and telling you about those guys fucking me, I had pretty well forgotten all about those actions, well, anyway, had tried to! But now things are kind of coming back to me, and with you standing there almost totally naked, and showing how that towel is sticking out in front, well, I'm kind of getting what I call 'ass hungry' again. I gotta be honest! Todd, I've not tried to forget those fuckings I got, even the rough ones. I've been horny for a dick in my ass for too damn long now! I gotta be honest and tell you that, yes, I've tried and tried to force myself to just forget about it, but I can't, and I've been trying to get fucked again for a long time now! Please fuck me man, please fuck me!"

As Jim explained to him what was happening, he was pinching Todd's nipple and at the same time reaching down and starting to rub the damp towel that was still kind of hiding, but not very successfully, Todd's hard-on.

"Jim – Jim. Do you know what you are doing here man?" Todd asked with some emphasis! "Jim are you sure you want to be doing this? I mean man, you are starting to get me all hot and bothered and wanting to play with you. Jim should I go get some clothes on? Jim, I don't want you doing anything that you are going to regret later!"

"Todd, from what I am feeling right not, I don't think I'm going to regret this at all! Not at all! About the only thing that I could regret right now, is if you say, 'No.' "

With that statement, Jim grabbed a hold of the towel and pulled it off of Todd's waist.

"Oh my God, Todd! That damn thing looks just like Randy's did. Todd, I want that! Oh Todd, please tell me you will fuck me – please!"

Todd was now standing there in rather a deep shock. He certainly did not expect this conversation to take such an unexpected turn, and he was now totally on, 'shelf display,' stiff hard-on and all, bare from top to bottom, and was feeling as if he was being fully presented for qualification and approval, to this hunk of a guy – a married guy, with two kids! He knew that while in any gay bar he could have, and probably would have, grabbed this hunk on the spot, but should he now? Todd kept thinking this was supposed to just be a visit by some guy that might be interested in renting the room, and now it looked like it was turning into much more of something like the script to one of the gay porno films, a totally hot, hot sex session with no pre-planning at all. That part, the no pre-planning part, was a total excitement, though! That part did excite Todd and he knew he liked that part of what was happening here so unexpectedly!

For more than a full minute, neither man said anything. Jim continued to pinch Todd's nipple, and had now reached down and had taken Todd's meat stick into his hand. That warm touch of Jim's strong construction man's hand, made Todd that much more expanded and stiff.

Todd stood there rather at attention and allowed his new acquaintance to explore his left nipple and now his raging hard-on, that he knew he truly did want to feel slide up into that hunk's tight ass – but he still felt like he needed to make sure Jim really understood the consequences of maybe some later negative feelings, about what had happened, if he did get fucked again.

Todd had been admiring his visitor, as Jim told his stories of his prior experiences, but in no way did Todd have any imagination that things were going to take this turn. He had completely accepted the fact that this young hunk of a stud was a married man, and simply had some prior experiences in his life that were now, days gone by. In no way, when he had asked Jim to tell him about his event in the dark alley, or his events while at the construction school, did he ever have any imagination that maybe this strong construction specimen might still be active in those ways. He did not ask Jim to tell him of his experiences in any attempt to intentionally get him all turned on with the idea of having sex with him. Todd knew that Jim was a married daddy, and he did not want to create any confusions in Jim's mind about what actions he should be involved in. He thought he was maybe helping Jim work out some negative feelings that he still held from his earlier years. He did not intend to put Jim in a position of needing to make new decisions about his own personal sexuality.

"Oh my God Jim! Jim, are you sure you know what you are doing, man? Jim, this whole conversation has kind of gotten out of hand here man! Jim, I did not mean to get you excited, man. Jim are you sure you know what you are doing? Jim do you know what you are asking for?"

Jim looked at Todd and exclaimed very assuredly, "Do I know what I am doing? Do I know what I am asking for? Hell yes I do! And all I can say right now is I hope like hell you want to fuck my ass as badly as I want you back there fucking me! Todd, I have not had any dick up in my ass for seven or eight years now, and for that entire time, I've been wanting some good stiff dick rammed back up in there, and man, you have the dick I want! Todd, I want you to fuck me and make me think that I've got Randy or that Bob guy, back up in my butt again! Todd, please fuck me, please!"

Todd was still in some shock, but at the same time, moving onto a state of happiness and pleasure as he was slowly realizing that this very unexpected Sunday morning visitor was being very realistic in knowing just what he was wanting, and he also had the guts to express it and being very straight forward in asking for it. He knew that Jim was remembering very fondly his days of having a guy shoot his juices up in his ass, and for seven or eight years now, he has been missing that experience. He knew that Jim was now praying that he was once again with some guy that would use his ass again, and let him relive his prior years and the experiences that he had not enjoyed for way too long.

"Jim, are you sure? Jim, I do not want you doing this if later you are going to wish you had never stopped in here! Jim, how sure are you this is really the right thing for you?"

As Jim squeezed Todd's rod, which of course made it even that much more stiff and erect, he looked Todd squarely in the eye and said, "Todd, I have driven down sleazy streets and dark alleys for years now just hoping to find some guy that looked okay enough that I could throw in the back of my truck and take out into the country someplace, so he could fuck the hell out of my ass. But every guy I ever found was some fairy type of a guy, weighed about four hundred pounds or was too damn old to probably even get it up anymore. Todd, I did not know I was coming to some gay guy's house this morning, but now that I am here, and now that I have this rod in my hand, I know damn well, what in the hell I am doing! I am begging for a fucking, and I want it now! Can we please? Please, Todd, will you fuck me, please!? Todd I've been wanting to get fucked for years now. Barbara just does not have the equipment I need slammed up in my ass again. Todd, I love her, but she does not have a dick to slam up in my ass, and I want to feel you up in me as deep as you can go! Please?"

As Todd heard the mere pleading in Jim's voice, he realized and accepted that Jim was being very honest and very straight forward in his earnest desires of wanting to feel a good dick back up inside of him again. He had convinced Todd that getting fucked was his honest desires and later he would not be angry at himself for doing it again. He said he would probably be more calm and satisfied with himself. He said that right now he was just real frustrated with himself that he had not been able to get fucked, and he was spending more and more time trying to find someone to fuck him.

Jim once again asked, "Please Todd, will you please fuck me?"

Todd extended his arm around Jim's waist and softly said, "Yes man, yes! I'll be more than glad to fuck you if that is what you want. You are one hot looking man, and knowing that I get to fuck you is going to be my pleasure.

If that's what you really want, then so do I! Sure I'll fuck your ass! Hell yes man, you look like you could be some real fun!"

Immediately Jim started to unbutton and remove his Levi's and pull off his T-shirt. Within only moments, he was as completely bareassed naked as Todd was.

Todd looked down at Jim's cock, took a hold of it, and asked. "Is it O.K. if I suck on that stick for a minute before we fuck?"

"Oh God yes!" Jim exclaimed! "Yeah, yeah please!"

Todd could tell that even without asking, that it had been a long time since Jim had played around with a guy. His excitement level was just about at the same peak as some guy that had dreamed of getting together with some other guy, and he is now finally getting to do it. Jim's youthful excitement of getting to play around again, reminded Todd of his very first time with a guy, and how excited and nervous he was when Greg, an older boy in his neighborhood, took his cock into his mouth for the very first time. As Todd remembered how his childhood friend Greg, had sucked him in so completely and sucked so strongly on his rod, Todd attempted to recreate that same action as if this was truly Jim's first suck job. Todd knew that Jim had been sucked on before. He had mentioned how he made Mat suck on it, but how Mat never liked doing it. Todd did not know if Jim had been sucked off by any other guys, other than Mat, and if not maybe this actually could be Jim's first good, true, anxious, strong, sucking session.

Suddenly Todd pulled off, looked up to Jim and asked, "Hey, has anybody other than that Mat ever sucked on you?"

"No – why?" Jim replied.

"Just wondering!" Todd quickly answered as he aimed Jim's cock back toward his mouth and immediately sank his mouth down on it as far as he could push. His face immediately hit the fuzz of Jim's crotch. Todd now knew that he was Jim's first man on his dick that really wanted to take it and use it for all it was worth. It had really never been sucked on good before!

As Todd worked on Jim's stiff meat, Jim was starting to realize that this sucking session was definitely turning out to be much more sensual and much more sexually exciting than the times that he had forced Mat to suck on it. He realized this time, what a good strong vacuum, of a grown and anxious man's deep throat, could really feel like. He knew that Todd liked sucking his cock, and obviously Todd had years of prior sucking experience to share with him and his dick. Jim was really enjoying this!

"Oh God man! Oh shit Todd! I thought getting fucked felt good! Oh man, this feels damn good too! Yeah Todd, Mat is the only guy that has ever sucked on it, and I can tell right now that he really did not do it right! Oh man – you feel so good!"

Todd enjoyed the feel of Jim's young and stiff seven inch rod in his mouth, and as he still remembered his first time getting sucked on by Greg, he continued to use as much force and vacuum on it as he could, so that Jim would always remember this as his first true sucking.

As he was getting sucked on, without realizing it, or doing it on purpose, Jim slightly stooped down, reached down, and took a nipple of Todd's in each hand, and after getting a pretty good grip on each tit, he started pulling quite hard and steady! This was turning Todd on! He was starting to get the essence that Jim was, or could be worked into, a sex playmate that wanted a little more than just the slight, soft, gentle way of sex. This realization definitely turned Todd on! He truly enjoyed the feel, of Jim pulling his nipples as hard and as firmly as he was doing. Jim truly was pulling them much harder than most men would enjoy. This definitely was Todd's way of play! A good display of strength from man to man! He was using Jim's dick to his pleasure, sucking, chewing and biting on it, and he liked it that Jim was also using parts of his playmate, for his own personal pleasures, although Todd was pretty sure that Jim was not even conscious of what he was actually doing. That part was exciting to Todd too. Todd liked the idea that Jim was pulling on his tits so hard, and was abusing his body, but was not even conscious of what he was doing. That simply indicated to Todd, that was Jim's natural way of playing and his inner, unknown, desires of playing that way! That was and always had been Todd's style of action. He knew that if he and Jim were to continue to share some sex times together, that if he took it rather slow and easy, he would be able to get Jim into some of the more manly actions of some good rough sex. Then thinking back about Jim's original session in the back alley – the first time when Jim got fucked by Randy and Mat – he then realized why Jim would be the type of a man to like it rougher. His first time was all rough sex, and now he mentally associated rough with sex. To Todd, that was okay! He really did not care why Jim unknowingly liked it rough, but the fact that he did, was a complete turn-on to Todd! If Jim could be worked into a 'true-player,' as Todd referred to the rougher actions, that would be great with him.

Realizing his new vision of Jim and perhaps what Jim liked, Todd decided that it definitely was time to throw that young man and his hot body down on the bed and let him have what he had been begging for so earnestly earlier. Todd thought, "I'm gonna fuck his ass! Oh yeah, and I am going to really, really fuck him! If it's too much, so be it, but I am going to find out just how rough he likes it back there! He hasn't shot off yet, and if I can keep him from shooting off until after I get in his ass, that will just make him that much more anxious for whatever I can give him! I'm going to fuck the hell out of him."

"O.K. guy! Time for me to get to your ass like you asked for! Ready for me to ram that butt of yours?"

"Oh God yes!" Jim exclaimed with anxiety and joy! "Oh God yes Todd! I've been wanting this for way too long! Todd, fuck me good – please!"

Once again Todd had heard the kind of words that he really liked hearing. Those rather – 'give it to me really rough,' – 'get kind of strong with me,' and 'make me really, really feel it!'

Jim quickly threw his body down on the bed, and in anticipation, Todd could watch Jim's ass jump up and down as if there were already somebody in there, poking and pounding around.

As Todd positioned himself above Jim's rump, he slid some KY jelly up into Jim's asshole, slid a couple of fingers up in to smear the jelly around good, and heard Jim exclaim, "Oh my God Todd – oh my God that is great! Are you fingering my ass? Are you putting your fingers up in my ass? Oh Todd, nobody has ever put their fingers up in my ass! Oh my God Todd that is great!! Oh yeah – oh do that some more!! Oh my God! Oh shit man that is great! Oh Todd how many fingers have you got up in me? Oh I've never felt anything like that before! Oh shit man – oh God that is great!"

"I've only got two fingers up in there. Like that, uh?"

"Oh my God yes I do! Oh shit man, if two fingers feel like that – what in the hell do three or four feel like up in there?"

"Hey man, I can tell you they feel great, even better than what you are feeling right now, but that's going to wait. My dick is getting real anxious to feel your asshole grab hold of it, so get ready man, how do you want it? Want me to kind of sneak up on it and go in real slow and nice like, or is your ass hungry and anxious for it as soon as it can get it? You want it slow and gentle or you want to take it like a real man?"

"Oh God Todd, fuck me like a real man! Todd slam your dick up in me! Fuck me man! Fuck me!"

Todd had gotten the answer that he had hoped for. The, 'Fuck me like a real man!' He knew his questioning had been kind of slanted toward the direction that he wanted. He had asked how Jim wanted it so that his answer could not be some little wimpy way of, slow and gentle.

Being secure that he had successfully gotten Jim's butthole sufficiently opened and relaxed for entry, Todd raised his torso up, aimed his rod, felt the tip of it hit the entry spot of Jim's asshole, and actually, after taking a rather deep breath, he instructed, "Hold on man! You are about to be fucked again!"

Before Jim had any opportunity of reply, if he did have any statements or questions, all he could do was let out a very large groan and moan, and somewhat of a pronounced squeal, since he had just taken the entire length and width of Todd's cock. For a moment he felt like maybe Todd had completely crawled up and into his ass. As Todd planted it to its fullest depth, he immediately laid down on Jim's back and threw his arms up around Jim's head and said, "Jim baby, you just got fucked! You are fucked! Totally fucked! You have got all of my dick up in you as far as I can push it! You are getting fucked my man! Give me your ass! I want to fuck your ass!!!"

Jim managed to get himself rather recomposed and back to a normal breathing pattern and attempted an, "I know, yeah, I am! Oh fuck yes – I am! Oh God this is what I need! Oh God yes! Fuck me! Fuck me!!!"

As Jim spoke, Todd literally started making hay in Jim's ass. Since Jim had spoken, he knew Jim was alright, maybe a little whipped and drained after the ass ramming that he had just taken, but none the less, he was okay and now he was going to just see what a, very experienced, ass fucker could do to a nice hungry ass that had done nothing except shit, for way too long. Jim had, unknowingly, let Todd know that his natural desire associated with gay sex was 'rough gay sex,' and he had just had his first true experience of it with a 'Master of the Trade.' Todd just did not think that any of the three young former fuckers, the ones that had used Jim's ass in the past, could have really given Jim the handling that he was so anxious for. Today, Jim was getting a true preview of real, man to man sex, as Todd felt that all gay sex should be. Todd knew that by the end of this session both he and Jim would know if Jim was, or was not, into some real man to man rough sex. No pansy stuff, but real man to man, let's get it on, type of sex!

Todd had experienced enough sessions in the past where the playmate was just too wimpy and too, 'Oh don't do that to me!' He truly enjoyed having a man under him that was a possible – true player! He just simply knew that Jim could be, and would be, labeled a true player, as he gained more and more experience. Todd knew that all men, that eventually became what he called a true player, just simply needed some time and some teaching to help him experience and learn some of the rougher, man on man, stuff that some playmates look for all of the time. He knew that a 'true player' and the more mellow players just simply did not make it as playmates. The 'true player' wanted and needed to be treated like a rough person, and he had the necessity of being able to treat his playmate as a man that could, and truly did want to take it the rough way!

Jim was actually getting it rougher and faster in his ass, than any other fucking that he had ever taken. He always thought his first time, the time in the back alley, had been rough, but today he knew he had a man in his ass that knew what in the hell he was doing and he knew how to do it with authority. The whole difference between the fucking in the alley and this day, was, number one, he trusted this fucker of knowing what he was doing, and number two, he had been fucked enough to know that however Todd treated his ass, when it was all over and done, he would actually be okay. He also knew that after this session, he just might have the feelings that he now belonged, totally and completely, to Todd, as if Todd had succeeded in taking a complete ownership over the item that he had just used to his complete enjoyment and pleasure. He knew that he and his ass were truly being used as perhaps, even a non-human object, to Todd's total excitement and pure joy and pleasure, and he was internally glad that he happened to be the guy that was letting Todd have that much fun. To be lying under the man, and to have the man use him and all of his body parts to reach such a great personal level of pleasure, was exciting to Jim. He knew that if he was not lying there, and making himself available to Todd, then Todd would not have had the opportunity to reach such blissful heights of personal bodily enjoyments.

Jim was wondering if Todd fucked this hard with all of his playmates, right when he unexpectedly got his answer. "Oh God Jim, I'm fucking the hell out of you! Shit man, I'm fucking you harder than I have fucked any guy's ass in years! You O.K. man? You O.K.? Oh Jim I love fucking this ass of yours like this! God you've got a great ass! You O.K.? You taking this O.K.? God Jim! I feel like I'm about to rip you all to shreds! You doing O.K.? Man, I feel like I'm about to pull my own dick off in your ass! Oh man, I've never fucked some guy's ass this hard before! God man, you doing O.K.?"

"Yeah man – yeah – I'm O.K. Yeah Todd, I'm O.K."

Jim felt that to get that much expressed, back to Todd, was a total accomplishment since he was having a very difficult time of attempting to talk at all. His body was in such a complete thrashing of getting fucked so roughly and so rapidly, that he just could only slightly catch his breath, let alone try to talk.

Jim reached out with each arm and grabbed the side of the mattress. He felt that unless he attempted to hold onto something, somehow, both of them could fly completely off of the bed the way Todd was fucking him! He spread his legs out so that his toes were pointing toward the corners of the bed. Todd grabbed hold of the under side of Jim's upper arms. He then slid his hands up and under Jim's arms and then grasped his own hands behind Jim's neck. He was giving Jim a wrestler's 'full nelson' body lock, and doing that, took complete body control of Jim. Being locked so completely to Todd's body, the way Todd did have them locked together, meant that Jim had lost all control of his own body movements and his body simply flew up and down as Todd's ramming and slamming, on him, and into him, forced him. Both bodies moved in union to whatever rhythm Todd used in his massive fucking force! Jim could not imagine any species of wild animal that fucked their mates as roughly, and as wildly, as he was now getting fucked by Todd! He liked that feeling. He actually liked the idea that he was now being treated more wildly than perhaps any other living thing. He had never considered the fact that maybe he needed to be treated and perhaps taken advantage of so completely and so roughly, but now that he was the man on the bottom and there was another man on top of him, and in-fact also inside of him, that feeling was great! It was more than he could imagine! He was now experiencing an emotion that he had never experienced before, nor had even contemplated before. He was, in his humorous mode – 'In Fucking Heaven!'

Jim knew that he had just lost any and all self-control, but he truly accepted this and was so disappointed that in this position he simply could not talk and tell Todd how great this was. He loved the feeling of being so completely locked up against Todd's body! The way he was pinned down under Todd's body made any attempts of movement or talking completely unsuccessful. He did not care though, as long as Todd kept it up and did not quit. His head was actually pouncing up and down on the pillow. His ass was slamming up and down every time Todd slammed into it or pulled out of it, and Jim wanted to cry in excitement, for how he truly loved this feeling of totally giving his entire body to Todd, for Todd to use and abuse, to any degree that he wanted. Jim had accepted the fact that right then he was no longer an individual person, but was rather an extension of Todd and Todd's existence. He knew that he and his whole body were being used! He realized that now he was nothing more than a trash can to be used and abused, in any way that this man wanted to use it! He liked the feeling. He knew he had submitted his entire being, and his entire body, to another man, and this excited him immensely! He knew that if it could be possible for Todd to stay locked to him like this for the rest of his life, and that if Todd could possibly keep up this rough fucking, for the rest of his life, this is the way that Jim would be spending the rest of his life. He knew that right then, all decisions would be Todd's decisions! Jim had completely turned his entire being, over to Todd and to Todd's control. And he was excited that he had been able to do that! He liked it! He knew now that this was the type of activity he had been aching for, ever since that very first time when Mat and Randy had fucked him. This fucking that he was getting this day was much more brutal than what had happened to him in the alley, but this time, there is no way he could call it being taken advantage of or being used! He decided that the only title he could give this session was, 'Finally!' He knew that it was not normal for a person to want to be treated this way, so extensively, nor to submit their entire being so completely, to another person, especially a person of the same sex, but he truly felt, as he mentally put it together, that he was now offering everything he had, including his most personal body parts to a 'King,' for that 'King' to do with as he so chose. He felt as if perhaps this might be the closest thing to actually offering yourself as a sacrificial lamb, for some reason. He was so overjoyed that he was able to offer Todd this opportunity of complete pleasure, that he was wishing that others could come and watch the action between him and Todd, so that they too could share, in some small way, the experiences and the pleasures that he was offering to his extremist fucker, and also be able to enjoy the excitements that the fucking man was accepting, for his total and complete pleasures!

He felt that what was happening, could possibly be the only time, in either one of their lives, that they had found such a complete physical and emotional satisfaction, of using another person, and that person's body parts for such a great fulfillment of personal joys! This session was truly turning out to be a session, unduplicated by others, wherever they were. This had become much more than just two men having a fucking session! This had turned out to be an event, when one man had submitted totally and completely, his entire body and being, to a man that he had only met a few minutes earlier. Yet, that man that had submitted his entire existence to this unknown person, had finally reached a pinnacle in his own life that was richer in emotions and excitements than he had ever expected to offer to, or receive from, any other person, for any reason or action.

Jim had wondered for years, of why he did not want to get Mat and Randy in trouble for fucking him, and getting so rough with him in the alley that night, and why he decided to keep it a secret. Now, as he was getting some body abuse, rougher than he had ever felt before, including that night, he was actually realizing that what had happened to him that night was actually something that he had internally wanted to have happen.

Now, getting fucked like some wild animal by Todd, he was not scared and he was realizing that he was sexually being treated the way he had always wanted to be treated. Now he wondered if unconsciously he had made comments to, or in front of Mat and Randy that indicated to them that maybe he wanted some guys to come and attach him, and he had never realized that he had perhaps actually, kind of told them to come and do him. He realized that if this was his true nature of desires, he could have very unconsciously made comments to those two guys that sounded like he was straight forward asking them to do that. He did faintly remember making comments to Randy about his big dick a few times while they were showering together in the school shower. He had pretty good ideas during those school days, that Mat and Randy did play around with each other, and now he wondered if he had made comments to those two guys that made them decide that getting him, would be okay. Now, he had serious questions about if he had actually, unknowingly, opened the door for those two guys to come and fuck him. Had he unknowingly demonstrated to them, or said something to them, that he could be open to getting fucked? The thought was intriguing to him. The thought that perhaps he had almost actually set up his own attack and 'abuse,' was not getting him upset at all. He was finding that idea very intriguing! The idea that during the rest of that time, when he made those two guys fuck him whenever he went to their dorm room, now he realized that maybe it wasn't so much as trying to make life hell for them, as much as actually getting his jollies by getting his ass fucked, and by the same guys that he thought had been so rough on him. He was finally deciding that getting fucked, in the alley and the other times too, was, and probably always had been, due to his internal desires and a result of his own unconscious actions, and not that of Mat nor Randy. Mentally, he wondered now, if he had managed to actually use Mat and Randy – unconsciously for his own unrealized desires. He used them – not that they had used him.

Suddenly, while he was still getting his ass pounded harder than if somebody had used a jack hammer on it, Jim had a realization that getting his ass fucked, and getting it as roughly as possible, was really a natural desire for him, and the actions of Mat and Randy were not to blame! It had always been his own natural desires. All of a sudden he realized too, that if he had not wanted it so naturally, he would, and could, have forced Bob to stay away from him, and he would never have asked Bob if he wanted to fuck his 'Little Rover' puppy. Even then, he had allowed himself to be verbally converted to a dog, letting the doggie ask for the fucking, instead of he, himself, admitting that he needed it up in the ass. Often he had questioned just why he had put up with Bob's drunken state of being, and now he realized that he actually did enjoy Bob being drunk, since that could mask his own personal desires for Bob to take advantage of him and his ass, and still claim that it only happened because Bob was drunk. Oh, how he now wanted to talk to Bob, to see if he had actually been that drunk all of those nights, or was he doing that, knowing that if he did not come home 'drunk,' that maybe Jim would not put out for him. He remembered that there were only a total of probably three nights when he had rejected Bob's pawing. Out of ten months, he had let, or maybe had encouraged, Bob to fuck his ass, all of the time thinking, that only he knew what was going on. Now he was quickly realizing that if Bob had really been that drunk each night, his getting out of bed and to class so early the next morning would have been a problem. He was suddenly deciding that most of the time, Bob was probably as sober as he was, but he liked getting into Jim's ass as much as Jim liked having him up in there, and he might have been afraid that if he did not act drunk, then Jim would not let him use his ass for someplace to deposit his nightly cum load!

For a moment Jim ponder the 'why' he would have, for so many years, continued the firm thinking that Bob had to have always been drunk, when in line with his now, new thinking about his actions, he suddenly realized that he had constantly been creating a line of reasoning, that always gave him other reasons for getting fucked, and never accepting the true reason, of him actually wanting it and needing it!

Suddenly Jim realized that getting it in the ass was only one action, of really many, many, that he wanted to do. Finally accepting the fact that his getting fucked had always been truly due to his own inner desires and wishes, and not the actions of others. He was now accepting the fact that he really did have many more desires of more sexual actions, that he really wanted to be part of. All of the rest of what he had fantasized about, he had tried to keep hidden from himself, as well as from everybody else. Suddenly he wanted some action in all of the gay stuff that he had read about, or heard about, in the past. Suddenly he wanted to have open and outrageous sex with any guy that he could! He wanted to experience everything that he felt that he had been missing.

As Jim was realizing his natural life and his true existence, suddenly Todd grabbed him tighter than he had before, used every muscle he had available to squeeze him as tightly as he could, and rammed his rod as deeply up into Jim's butt as he could and just held that position.

"Oh my God man!!! Oh God!!! Oh Jim – oh Jim – I'm cummmmmmmmmin man! I'm cummmmmmin!" Todd's body functions had just kicked in, and he was almost screaming into Jim's ear!

Jim knew that Todd was quickly becoming a man of stone, as his entire body locked into a rigid position, and as he released his sperm into Jim's ass!

Jim felt, what actually felt like a gallon, of warm fluid hit the inside of his ass. He had never felt such warm cum hit the inside of his body! Even the first night in the alley when, he had been left with both Randy's cum and Mat's cum dripping out of his ass, did it feel this warm. Todd's cum felt like it had been put on the stove to warm to a point almost at boiling!

"Oh yeah Todd! Oh yeah I can feel it! Oh Todd it is so damn warm! Oh man push on me! Oh Todd, push your cock up in me as far as you can. Oh man it feels so good to me!"

Both men were in a complete state of glory as Todd let his juices fly, and as Jim accepted them into his 'inner chambers.'

"Oh God Todd, I've got part of you up in me! Oh Todd, I love that man, I love that. Oh man, I don't ever want to take another shit man. I wanna keep your cum up in me!"

Jim and Todd laid together, still locked together for another two or three minutes before Todd loosened his grip on Jim's body and slowly rolled over to allow Jim to rather breathe, without having a man lying on his back.

"Oh Todd! Oh man I never knew it till right now how I loved getting fucked so damn hard that I couldn't do anything but lie there and take whatever happened to me! Todd that was a lot rougher than anything I have ever taken, even the time in the alley. Oh, I loved that! This time I knew that no matter how rough you got back there, I'd be okay and nothing was going to get all ripped up, and I loved that! Todd there must be something wrong with me to like having my body treated that way. I kept wanting you to get rougher and rougher the longer we fucked! Todd, I wanted you to turn into some kind of a machine that could just get faster and faster, and let me get fucked faster and faster. I know, that's kind of sick, isn't it? Nobody is supposed to be like, that are they?"

"Hey Jim my man! I don't know if anybody is supposed to be or not, but let me tell you, I'm another one just like you. I fucked you as hard and as fast as I could, and the whole time I was wanting to go deeper, faster and harder than I could. I wanted to make you squeal and make you tell me that you'd had enough, but Jim my man, I'm not sure you nor I, either one, will ever hit our limit of being enough. I love to play with you. I have not had a good, 'beat me up and beat my ass up,' guy to play with, for way too long. And when I say beat – I mean with my dick. Just getting to use my dick in him as hard and as long as I can! I guess that's why I'm not in a long term relationship. I've never been able to find some guy that wants to play as rough as I do. Seriously Jim, you are the first guy in years that I just knew, when I started, that I could ram your ass as hard and as deep as I could for as long as I could. Yeah, I wanted to turn into some kind of a fucking machine too! I wanted to ram your ass twice as hard and twice as fast as I could! I fucking love, fucking you! You have got one hungry asshole! You know Jim, a guy that gets fucked, and likes to get fucked long and rough, can always get a whole line of guys ready to do him when one guy gives out. I know you've never done it, but the way you love to get it in the ass, you are the type of a guy that needs to get about five guys together, and then get fucked by each one of them, and as fast as one gets off in you, and off of you, you get another one, up and in you! Damn man, I sure am glad you insisted that we play! Damn I am glad! God you are fun stuff to pay with!"

"Oh Todd! Oh God man! Oh shit man – is that possible to do that? I mean get a whole group of guys together at the same time to fuck a guy that way? Oh shit man, I'd love that! God, do guys do that? Oh Todd, I'd never ever thought about something like that! Oh man! Oh God man, I want to do that! Oh man! Talk about being used! Oh shit man, I'd love that! Oh Todd, can you help me get that many guys together to do that? Oh Todd please say yes!"

"Hey, I'm not promising anything. I've had enough trouble finding my own guys to play with. I'm not making promises that I can do that. Maybe so, if everything goes right, maybe it could happen, but I sure can't promise things I'm not sure of. One thing that I do know right now though is, I'm going to go get you some paper towels to put up against your ass so you can get into the shower. Don't turnover yet, cause I know that if you do, cum is going to come flowing out of your ass, since I am sure I shot more than just a little bit of it up and in you. Lie there and I'll be right back."

Jim stayed on the bed, stomach down until Todd returned with a couple of paper towels which he slid up into Jim's ass so that he could stand up and get to the shower without dripping cum all over the bed and the floor.

Todd suggested to Jim that he use the flexible shower head and kind of shoot some water up in his ass to clean out some of the cum that had been deposited up in there, so that it didn't come running out later. He told him to, 'Flush your ass out some.'

Jim showered and Todd straightened the bed covers since they had never been folded down before the two anxious and horny men got onto it.

Jim got out of the shower and Todd gave him a bath towel to use, and after drying off some, Jim started to get re-dressed.

Todd turned the shower water on and stepped into the shower to start his shower.

Just as Todd was letting the water flow over him, Jim yelled to him, "Hey Todd, somebody is ringing the front doorbell. Want me to answer it or what do you want to do?"

Todd yelled back, "Yeah, it's probably Jerry and George, a couple of friends that I was expecting this morning, but if it's somebody concerning the ad, what're you going to tell them?"

"Hell man, I'm going to tell them it's already rented – O.K.? Can I tell them that!"

"Hell yes you can! That is what I was wanting to hear! Yeah – answer the door."

With only his Levi's partly buttoned and his shoes on, no shirt yet, Jim did answer the door and was confronted with the presence of two very attractive men. Jim simply asked, "Yes?"

The hunk on the left, about age thirty-two or thirty-three, six foot one or close to, and at about a hundred and ninety-five pounds of all steel, solid, muscle, and the sharpest and squarest jaw that Jim had ever seen, spoke up and said, "Uhhhh – I'm Jerry. Is Todd here?"

Immediately Jim realized that this had to be the two friends, Jerry and George, that Todd had so quickly mentioned just might be the person ringing the front doorbell.

"Oh, Hi!" Jim replied. "You are Jerry and George, right?"

Jerry rather hesitantly replied, "Yeahhhhh, and you are – – – ?"

"Oh I'm sorry!" Jim quickly replied. "I'm Jim. Come on in guys, Todd is in the shower. He told me it might be you two. He said he was expecting you guys."

Jim opened the screen door and allowed the two men to come into the house. Jerry definitely looked Jim over as he walked by, and George, the other hunk of a man, did the same.

George was slightly older, perhaps in his early to mid forty's, stood about five feet ten inches tall, a little less muscular than Jerry, but none the less, a very athletic type of a guy.

Jerry extended his hand and again said, "Hi, I'm Jerry and this is George!"

Jim shook hands with both men, and then after greeting them, asked them to come on in, and informed them that Todd would be right there, since he was just getting into the shower as they rang the doorbell.

"Excuse me guys! I need to go find my shirt. I guess I forgot just where I threw it."

As Jim left the room, Jerry looked at George, raised his eyebrows, grinned, and then licked his lips. George returned the same exact actions. Each man then silently looked at each other with a very quick, quizzed look on each of their faces. None the less though, they both then smiled a very wide smile as they watched the ass end of Jim, walking down the hall toward the bedroom. Each man shook his head up and down a couple of times. They definitely did approve of what they had just seen. Confused, yes – but definitely approved!

George looked at Jerry and silently pointed to his ring finger of his left hand and made a motion of, "Did you notice he had a wedding ring on?"

Jerry silently made a strong facial expression of, "Oh?" He then made an animated expression of, "Wow!" and followed it with a very large grin, and then a thumbs up signal! Jerry and George definitely were in step and agreement, that Jim, 'obviously,' had not just stopped by to deliver the Sunday morning, church bulletin. That was for sure!

Room For Rent
Chapter Four:
And My Levi's Only Partly Buttoned

Todd finally came into the living room, finishing up on putting his shirt on.

"Hey guys, good morning! How you both doing?" he asked as he grabbed each man, pulled him up tight and gave him a hug. "How's everything?"

Looking at Todd, and then rather leaning forward some as if to look down the hallway some, Jerry said, "Uh – O.K.! With us anyway." Then leaning in toward Todd, and with a big grin on his face, he whispered, "So tell us, how's everything with you?"

Realizing what Jerry was meaning, Todd rather laughed and said, "Oh! Ah, kinda guess maybe you are wondering about the new guy! Right?"

Jerry looked at Todd, grinned and shook his head "Yes," quite frantically! George did the same.

"I decided that I wanted to rent out the extra room just so I'd have somebody around here once in awhile, and Jim stopped by this morning to see what was available, and so, anyway, he's the new tenant."

"The new tenant!?" Jerry almost too loudly exclaimed. "The new tenant? From what I saw a few moments ago, I'm not so sure the word tenant, is the full description!"

"Well guys, things did kind of take a different turn once he was here.

See, I did not know the ad was gonna be in today's newspaper. I was told it probably would not hit the paper until tomorrow. When Jim got here and rang the door bell, I was in the shower. I actually thought it was you guys ringing the door bell, but it was him instead. I came to the door with just a wet towel wrapped around me. After that, things kind of got out of control. After he acted kind of interested in the place, then I did tell him that I am gay, just so he would know that once in awhile there might be some activity going on around here, and from that point on – well just let me say, that it has been, well had been, quite some time since the married daddy has had a chance to let someone push his rod up in him! We – I guess – kind of lost control this morning, and he told me that he needed to be fucked, and I gave it to him. And I will tell you guys, he fucks! Well anyway, he gets fucked rough! He is the kind of a fuckee that I've been looking for, for a long time. He fucking exhausted me and kept wanting more!"

"Uh, Todd!" Jerry rather interrupted. "If he's married, and he's renting out your room, does that mean that he and his lady are separating or something?"

"No, no! He lives down in Woodville and it's just too far away from Denver to be driving every day, so he's renting out the room so he can stay in town during the week. He's working construction on a big apartment complex over on the east side of town."

"Uh, O.K.! So he's a married man, probably a daddy, and all of a sudden when he stops in here to see about a room, he gets fucked! Right?"

"Well yeah, I guess. A little more involved than that, but yeah."

As Jim walked into the room, Todd again introduced the two to him, on a much more formal basis than what had happened at the door, and then asked, "So Jim. What do you wanna do? I assume you don't have your stuff with you, do you?"

"No, no I don't. If it's O.K. with you, what I thought what I'd do, is go back to the motel, get my stuff, get checked out of there before the one PM deadline, and then come back over here. Is that O.K. with you? Does that work O.K.?"

"Jim, that is perfect! I've gotta give you a key. Don't let me forget that before you leave, and when you get back, then we'll kind of get you all settled in some. O.K.?"

"Yeah, O.K.!" Then looking over toward Jerry and George, Jim asked, "Uh – Todd! I assume you have kinda explained to them that I'll be around here some during the weekdays, right?"

"Yeah Jim, I did. I told Jerry and George that I'm renting out the extra room so that I'd have some company in the house once in awhile!"

"Uh, did you happen to tell 'em why I met them at the front door with no shirt on and my Levi's only partly buttoned?"

Grinning some, Todd looked over at Jerry and George and said, "Yeah Jim, I did. They already knew something had happened just before they got here. I mean, you half dressed, and me in the shower, so yeah, I leveled with 'em. They know you're a married daddy, but they're also smart enough to know that once in a while, or maybe once in a decade, a man just needs the services of another man, and that is what happened here today."

Then turning to the two, Todd asked, "Right guys?"

Both men agreed, "Right!" Then George added, "And right now I can see that Todd is smiling a hell of a lot bigger than normal, so I kind of guess maybe he needed those services too. Right, Todd?"

"You are damn right man, damn right! Hey Jim, here is the key to the front door so you can get back in if we are not here when you get back, but we probably will be since we're planning on just spending the day in the pool and drinking some Buds."

"The pool!!?" Jim suddenly asked. "You have a pool!?"

"Oh yeah, yeah! I guess I never mentioned that did I? A pool in the back yard, and I've got a pool table in the rec room in the basement. I kinda guess that when you get back from the motel, I need to give you a guided tour of what's around here."

With a big smile on his face, Jim replied, "Yeah! Yeah, I guess so! I had no idea you had a pool and I didn't even know there was a basement and a pool table down there. Hey, got a question."

"Yeah, what?"

"If you guys are gonna be in the pool this afternoon, where's a good place, close to here, that I can stop and buy some swim trunks? I don't have any with me. I never thought I'd be needing swim trunks while in town."

"Uh, Jim, it's up to you, but in my pool, you really do not need trunks. If you feel better using trunks, that's O.K., but I gotta warn you, none of the rest of us ever wear any, so whatever you decide. Don't waste the money on 'em if you don't feel like you really, really gotta have 'em."

Looking over toward Jerry and George, Jim just rather expressed a facial expression of some confusion and shrugged his shoulders. Jerry quickly added in, "Hey man. No trunks, O.K.? I know Todd's already seen it, and all the rest of us are just gonna be guys, and we've all got one that is gonna hang out there, so just do the natural thing. Let it fly!" Then looking at Todd, Jim just uttered a smiling, "Oh, O.K. Guess I will then."

Todd then took Jim into his home office and gave him a note with his cell phone number on it for a 'just in case' situation, and he in turn, then wrote down Jim's cell phone number, so that he'd have it also.

As Jim went past the living room, he waved at Jerry and George, and yelled, "I'll see you guys in just a little while. All I gotta do is grab a suitcase, throw some stuff back in it and then get checked out. Be back soon." And with that, left and headed back to the motel.

And with Jim now out of the house, and not within earshot, Jerry and George were much, much more than anxious to hear all of the details about Jim showing up, unexpected, and what in the world had happened to have the two end up in bed together so quickly, and of course, how the fucking was.

"Men, I gotta tell you, that man is an animal when he is getting fucked. You know me well enough to know that I've fucked a little more than my share, but this man is a fucking wild animal! He fucking exhausted me, he did!"

"Did he fuck you, or just you fuck him?" George asked with interest.

"No, I just fucked him. I gotta be honest, I'm not sure if he has ever fucked some guy or not. While he was in the construction school, his roommate always acted drunk and was always wanting to fuck him, but I'm not sure if Jim has ever fucked some guy or not! He's told me about two guys getting to him in a dark alley one night, and then the guy at construction school fucking him, but I don't remember him saying anything about him fucking some other guy! Hey, maybe I will be able to get him to fuck me, and then I can be his first piece of ass – if he's never fucked some other guy!"

"Well, did he know this was a gay household when he came over to see the place? When did he get here?" George asked.

"Well, he got here right about ten, and like I said, I did not even know the ad was in the paper yet. No, there was no mention about this being a gay household. That came out when I wanted to be sure he would be comfortable living in a house that would have gays running around, probably naked some of the time. It was while we got to talking about that, that he started telling me about his night out in the alley and what had happened to him, and then how he kept it up until he got married. I was standing there with just a towel wrapped around my – well should I say – my excitable parts of my body."

Almost jumping up and almost yelling, Jerry interrupted with, "What!!? All you had on was still just a towel wrapped around your waist? Is that what you just said? You never went in and put any pants on!? The whole time you guys talked about him renting a room here, all you ever had on was a wet towel!?"

"Well yeah. Everything just went that way! At first I was gonna go get dressed, but then it just never happened. And then when he was telling me about how he had been fucked by those two guys, and then the construction guy that kept calling him 'Rover' and fucking him, I got hard and it stuck out like a tent, and then Jim pulled my towel off, grabbed my dick and told me he wanted me to fuck him."

"So just like that, you took him into the bedroom and fucked him, right?"

"I kept asking him if he was sure that, that was something he wanted to do, and he kept telling me yes. He told me how he's been wanting to get fucked for about seven years now, and he's even gone out and driven around trying to find someone to do it, but he never found anyone. Yeah, he wanted fucked. And he wanted fucked hard and rough! And he got it hard and rough."

"Uh Todd. Did he suck you any, or did you suck on him any?"

"I sucked on him a little bit, and he told me that he had made one of the back alley guys suck on him while the other guy fucked him. That was while he was at the construction school and those two were at a junior college, rooming together in a dorm. That was when Jim gained control over those two and made them fuck him and suck him whenever he wanted it."

"So guys, anyway, we had just managed to get up and try to get reorganized when you guys showed up. I had Jim take the first shower since he had some of my man juices running down his leg, and that's why he was out of the shower when you guys got here. That's it! That's what happened this morning! Rented out the room damn fast didn't I?"

Jerry looking at Todd then softly stated, "Yeah, yeah I'd say so. And from what I know so far, you might have rented out your bed pretty fast too. You guys gonna be doing the ole fucking thing a lot while he's here?"

"Jerry, I don't know. I really don't. I gotta admit I think maybe Jim has got some life living decisions to make. Once he was here, and he found out I was a gay guy, he just went almost bananas about wanting to get fucked again."

George then interrupted with, "Well of course he did man! For God sakes man! Look at what he was looking at! Hell, a lot of straight men have probably turned gay just looking at you, or maybe, have even been fucked by you, even though you never knew they were straight! You got one hell of a hot body man! I don't blame him any – at all – for going for it, especially if all you had on was a wet bath towel. Hell, that'd make some ole woman Baptist minister turn gay too."

Room For Rent
Chapter Five:
Some Learning To Do Here

Jerry looked at Todd and asked, as he got out of the pool to grab a beer and some chips, "Hey Todd, I just heard someone in the house. Is that Jim?"

Todd looked toward the house and then answered, "I guess so. Hey, I'll be right back. I probably ought to go see if I can help him any." And with that statement, Todd pulled himself up out of the pool, grabbed a towel, wiped his body somewhat dry, and dabbed a few times at his exposed dick and crotch hair. He then wrapped the towel around his waist, as he had done earlier in the day, and went into the house.

"Hey Jim! Get everything done O.K.? Get checked out of the motel O.K.?"

"Yeah, yeah sure did. And I will be glad to tell you that I am glad to be out of that place. I called Barbara and gave her the information about what is going on." Then with a big grin on his face, he quickly added, "Well, NOT ALL of the what is going on. Just the part about finding someplace that I can use during the weekdays. She was pretty happy, knowing that I've found a place to stay."

"Good! So she knows that you're not going to have to use some sleazy ole motel downtown to stay in, right? Funny things can happen there!"

"Yeah, right. And at about forty five dollars a night, and not being a good place anyway, the ole motel thing would have been really undoable. I didn't tell her though, of what you are gonna charge me for using your place. Guess maybe I need to come up with some good reason, or maybe a false dollar figure to tell her. If I'm gonna save the money, I'd better not tell her the truth. Well – about the money – and some of the other 'benefits' that I might get while I'm here, too."

Todd grinned, kind of tapped Jim on the shoulder indicating he agreed, and then said, "Hey, Jerry, George and Mike are outside. You haven't met Mike yet. He stopped in after you left. Come on out and I'll introduce you to him."

As the two men stepped out to the pool area, Todd did say, "Hey guys, Jim is back. Mike, this is Jim, and Jim, this is Mike."

Mike, a twenty-four year old, short flat top haired mechanic, with biceps that truly were as large as one-half of a big sized cantaloupe – came up to the edge of the pool and extended his hand out to shake hands. Jim reached down, took one great big breathe – once he saw the enormous arms – then quickly wished that he would be 'accidentally' pulled down into the water, and on top of Mike. The size of his biceps really did make it look like maybe he just lifted car engines up and out of the car, with his bare hands. He shook hands with Mike, and said, "Hello. Glad to meet you." Silently and mentally, he added, "And how I want to do more with you than just meet you!" Then looking over toward Jerry and George, Jim added, "Hi guys! How's the water?"

"Damn good!" Jerry replied. "We've got some Buds and some chips over there for any guy that jumps in and does some swimming, so strip it off and jump in here man!"

"Hey sounds good to me! Give me just a couple of minutes to put my suitcase in the room and I'll be out." Then looking at Todd, he added, "Hey, did not know exactly what you guys were planning today, but I sure do hope you've got some freezer room available, cause I stopped and got a couple of large pizzas so we could munch on 'em later. That O.K.?"

Todd looked at him and said, "Hell yes man, hell yes! You just didn't get any with anchovies on 'em, did you?"

"No! No! I can't stand anchovies so I never buy pizza with anchovies."

"O.K. – just checking! You know guys like us, well meaning the other four of us, we just don't like fish, so we kinda stay away from anchovies."

Looking somewhat confused as just to what Todd was commenting about, Jim simply uttered something like, "Uh, O.K.!"

Todd then reached over, patted Jim on the shoulder and said, "You'll catch on later. I gotta remember we've got a guy here now that may need some slight explanations until he catches up to all of the slang comments we make. See, guys like us, the happy, gay type of guys, we refer to women as 'fish.' Got it!?"

"Oh, oh! O.K., got it man, got it. I got me some learning to do here, don't I?"

"Yeah, but that's O.K.! Come on guy, let's go inside and kinda get you a little settled. I'll show you where to find some stuff – like maybe a towel or two – just in case you don't feel like putting all of your body on full display, quite yet. O.K.?"

As Todd and Jim went into the house, George looked over at Jerry and said, rather emphatically, "Man did you see the legs on that guy! When we saw him earlier he didn't have shorts on, he had long pants on and those calves were not showing. You may have some muscle competition going on here man! He didn't have a shirt on earlier, and I noticed he does have one hell of a nice chest, but man – those legs look like they are about as strong as the legs of some water tower!"

"Hey guys!" Mike added. "Guys, none of you even suggested to me that he is as hot as he is! You guys saw him earlier without a shirt on, and you never told me he's built like a brick shithouse? He is gonna join us swimming naked, ain't he?"

"Yeah, I think." George replied. "Before he left earlier, Todd told him he didn't need to go buy any swim trunks anyplace, since we all just swim in the nude, so I guess he's gonna."

"Well, he had damn well better," Mike expressed with some force! "I wanna see all of that!"

Inside of the house, Todd and Jim first put the pizzas in the freezer so they did not thaw out, and then they went into Jim's new room of residence and put his suitcase and some other items in there. Todd looked at Jim and asked, "Well man – did you see all of the eyes looking at you when you came out back? Of course Mike had never seen you before, but I certainly did notice Jerry and George checking out those legs of yours and those shorts. I guess earlier today they didn't get to see the legs, and from all of the looks that I just saw, I'd kinda guess they are both pretty well taken with what they just saw. I think Mike was pretty well taken by 'em too, but we'll have to see what he says when we go back out. You are still planning on joining us in the nude – right?"

"Yeah, yeah, I guess. Jim, I gotta admit, it's been years and years – hell, probably ten or fifteen years – since I've gone skinny dipping any, and I know I'm gonna feel pretty weird out there all bareassed and naked. I gotta be honest and tell you, I'm kinda afraid this thing is gonna start getting a little excited and react, when it's looked at. But I'll try."

"Hey good man, good. Just remember, you sure did not have any trouble with that this morning, and it's just more guys. O.K.?"

"Yeah, yeah. Maybe what I need to do is hit the water just as soon as I get out there and kind of hide everything for awhile."

"Hey, tell you what! Maybe this will help. Get undressed while I'm in here. I'll drop my towel so I'm bareassed too, and then it won't be just you."

Hearing what Todd was saying, Jim did pull off his shirt, take off his shoes and socks and then finally pulled off his shorts and his briefs.

"There! That better?" Todd asked as he stood there and looked at Jim's fully, completely nude body. "No different than earlier today, is it?"

"No, I guess not. But, it's not gonna be just you and me now. There's three other guys out there that I need to try and act like they're not around, and are not looking at my rod. I'm just not used to that! It's been years and years since gym class in school, and that was the last time I was with a bunch of guys all at the same time, and all of us naked. And besides, then everybody was looking at each other, but I know damn well that today when I go out there, at least for a few minutes, what I'm hanging between my legs is gonna be the center of attention. Right?"

"Well maybe, but then Jim, maybe you need to remember you've got a hell of a lot more to look at, than just your dick. You are one hell of a hot built guy, and yeah, they are gonna be checking you out, and to be honest, I will be too. Yeah, we pretty well rolled in the hay this morning, but I didn't get too much of a chance to really check out your whole body, so yeah, I'm gonna be looking at that physic, too. Come on! Let's go hit the pool and grab a beer. Oh, hey! You do drink beer, I assume. I never asked. I just kinda decided on my own, that you do."

"Yeah, I do. One of my more manly actions, I guess."

"No, no, no! No man! You need to remember back just a couple of hours ago! That was one of your more manly actions! That was truly man to man! And I do mean in a big way! And I gotta be honest, I'm not sure I ever thanked you for that! You really are the fuckee type of a guy that I like to fuck! Thanks man! You're not upset you did that this morning, are you?"

"No I'm not. Todd, I told you that I had been trying to get that done to me again for a long time, but I just kept trying to deny it. No man. This morning was something that I've needed for a long time."

"O.K., come on – let's go join the rest of the group. Oh hey! Another one is expected to show up sometime soon. He had to go to church this morning, so he's not here yet. His name is Rawl. He's a black guy, and a great guy to have around. Come on, let's go."

As the now, both bareassed, naked men came back out to the pool area, of course all eyes were on Jim, on his chest, his arms, his legs, his butt and of course on his dick.

Both men dropped their towels on a chair back and as Jim stepped down the steps into the water, Todd stepped up onto the diving board and did a dive into the deep end. Jim watched him in shock and surprise, and as quickly as he pounced up out of the water, Jim did ask, "Oh my God Todd, doesn't that hurt your balls when you dive in naked!?"

Rather grinning some, Todd replied, "No, not really. Well, maybe a little, but not too much! It's kind of fun."

"Fun like hell!" George chipped in. "Jim, don't do it! Talked me into it once and it hurt my nuts like crazy! Don't do it! I grabbed my nuts and held 'em for the rest of the day."

"But," injected Jerry, "you got tender nuts, and besides – that day you just needed a reason to hang onto your balls. It gave you a good excuse."

"Oh yeah man, I ain't seen you doing any bare ball nut diving!" George replied. "You ain't diving with your nuts hanging out, are you?"

"O.K., so maybe a little, but then you know as well as I do how our buddy Todd there likes everything as rough and tumble as he can get it."

And then without realizing just what he was doing, Jim grinned a big grin and shook his head, "Yes." Jerry saw it. He grinned back and then asked, "Jim, am I right? I know what happened this morning, am I right?"

All of a sudden Jim took a dive under the water, and everybody knew that was his way of not answering the question.

Slowly Jim got a little more adjusted and accustomed to being in the 'out and open' fully naked with other men around. That was until Jerry happened to look up from standing at the edge of the pool just as Jim walked by. Jerry's face and Jim's dick were actually only a few inches apart. All of a sudden Jim felt as if perhaps he was on display, and his dick reacted. Jerry noticed, and he grinned, and then he asked Jim, "Hey man, why'd that thing start jumping up like that? You like having a man's face up close to that rod?"

And with that comment and question, Jim immediately jumped into the pool, in a lame attempt to hide what was now becoming an unexplainable hard-on.

As Jim jumped into the water, Jerry laughed and asked, "Uh, that thing gets pretty big don't it?"

Being now rather embarrassed, Jim tried to deny it, but Jerry continued to be interested and said, "Hey guy, don't be embarrassed. A good big long one is the best. For with a gal, or for being with a guy. Come here man, let me see what you are hanging there."

With that comment of instruction, Todd slightly interrupted and said, "Hey Jerry. Maybe not, O.K.? I promised Jim that we wouldn't be doing any of our 'funny stuff' to him or with him, so let's not push it, O.K.?"

Jerry then looked at Todd and reminded him of what they knew had already happened earlier in the day. "Uh Todd my dear man! I kinda think what you promised this guy and what the realities are, are not really combining very well. Remember you told us about what went on this morning. Just maybe our man is a little more receptive to being admired than you think." Then looking at Jim, he asked, "Right man, am I right?"

Jim did listen to what had been said, and without realizing it, he had unconsciously reached down and grabbed his own cock and then his balls. Jerry saw the action. Mike also saw what had happened, and he stepped in a little closer. His simple movement toward the action would be a strong indicator that he was not going to be left out of any action, if something was going to get started.

Stepping over one step closer to Jim, which put Jim and his basket area within an arm's reach, he did reach out, and replaced Jim's hand, with his own. He looked up at Jim's face and simply saw Jim looking down and watching his cock and balls being handled. He said nothing until Todd rather said, "Jerry!!" Then Jim looked over at Todd and said, "It's O.K. Todd, really, it's O.K. Fact is, I gotta tell you, it feels good. Don't worry. It's O.K."

With that statement, Jerry broke out with a big smile, looked at Todd and then George, and said, "And men – it feels good to me too. Shit man, he must like this, it's getting stiff! In-fact, real stiff!" Then looking back at Jim, he simply smiled and squeezed his handful of man meat and nuts a little more firmly. He watched Jim's face brighten. He was silently being told that Jim was liking what he was feeling, and he was not asking for anything to stop.

As Jim got harder and harder, Jerry then looked over toward George and Mike and said, "Hey! Wanna feel something nice, real nice? This man has got a total crotch full of meat and it feels good. Come here guys. Grab it. Feel it. It is nice – real nice." Then he looked at Jim, and asked, "It's O.K. if George and Mike feels this pole ain't it?"

Jim did not reply, nor respond, but in such a way as to indicate that letting George and Mike grab onto it, was quite O.K. In fact, as he watched

George step over close enough, he realized that Todd and Mike were moving in that direction also. George replaced Jerry's hand, and then only moments later, Todd replaced George's hand, and at the same time, Mike was rubbing Jim's back, his butt cheeks, and down along the inside of his legs. That is when Todd looked at Jim and asked, "Hey man. I was on this for just a little while this morning, and honestly I didn't get enough of it then – so since you're letting all of us grab it, you willing to let me go back down on it for a few more sucks?"

Jim just looked at Todd, and without saying anything, and unknowingly, wet his lips – as if he was going to be doing the sucking – he simply shook his head and quietly said, "O.K."

Very silently and without words, Todd guided Jim into the more shallow end of the pool – where it was shallow enough that Jim's crotch would be above the water – he placed a hand on each side of Jim's hips and took the nine and a half, or ten incher into his mouth. Jerry and George both stood by and admired the actions, and the sight of Jim's big dick. Mike was a little more active, and as he stood by, he reached back behind Jim, and did a little finger playing, up in Jim's ole rosebud hole. That action 'forced' Jim to slightly push his torso forward to Todd, and into Todd's mouth. Jim let out a slight, "Oh yeah."

Simply standing there and watching, Jerry very calmly stated, to nobody in particular, "Long and thick! Look how thick that thing is! Looks like a dick off of some bull somewhere." Then looking at Jim, he asked, "You fuck guys with that thing?"

Jim looked over at Jerry and simply said, "No. Never have."

And with that, that is when Todd pulled off of his sucking for just a moment and said, "Said he never has, but men, there can always be a first time for anything!" He then immediately resumed sucking on the nine or ten inches – or whatever the real length was.

Mike continued to finger fuck the hole, combined with grabbing and squeezing both of Jim's firm butt cheeks. Jerry and George realized that obviously this activity was rather turning them on, since each man was now grabbing, jerking and pulling on his partner's dick.

"Hey, what in the hell is going on here guys?" Rawl stated with some surprise and excitement as he came out the back door of the house.

Everyone in the pool suddenly turned and realized that Rawl was there, although none of them actually knew for how long.

Todd pulled off of the rod, Jim and Mike looked over toward the voice, and George and Jerry turned far enough to realize what was happening.

Everybody gave their individual type of a 'Hi' or 'Hello,' and Rawl then added, "I kinda think maybe I was not informed of all of the details about today's pool party!" Then looking at Jim, he added, "Uh -, Hi! I'm Rawl. From what I see right now, it kinda looks like maybe you are the reason this party is a little different than usual. How are you?"

Quickly, Todd introduced Rawl and Jim, and did simply explain that Jim was going to be renting the extra room while working in Denver. The introduction was then finished up with, "Come on man. Pants off! Get in here with the rest of the gang. Can't have you standing up there looking like some Sunday School teacher – all tucked out in your Sunday finest!"

It did not take Rawl a second instruction to shed his clothes! Within only seconds he was displaying it all. Yes, all! All eleven inches of one beautiful, black man, thick and beautiful rod. Not even hard and stiff yet, it was outstanding! It was the Crème de la crème, of body parts. All Jim could think of for a few seconds, was, 'My god man, that is the body of a bronze God! That man is beautiful! Oh shit man, if this playing around goes any farther, I gotta let that guy do something to me and I hope like hell it is fuck me! God he is beautiful! Fucking beautiful!'

Rawl did a dive from the diving board. Once again there were expressions of pain from George and Mike. The diving 'bare nutted' was okay with Todd and Jerry, but the idea of the pain in the nuts, was just a little too much to think about for George and Mike. Jim simply could not have any opinion about the subject since he had never dove in, 'bare nutted,' but he had decided he wanted to ask Rawl if it did hurt or not. He knew he wanted to 'get close' to Rawl. He liked what he saw!

Just as Rawl surfaced to the top of the water, Jim looked over at him and said, "Damn man! I've never dove in 'bare nutted' like that before, but it's gotta hurt don't it? I watched your bag hit the water, and man, I'd think that's gotta hurt. Don't that hurt?"

Rawl moved over closer to Jim and Mike, who was still playing with Jim's ass, and stated, "No, not really! I guess if your balls are really sensitive then maybe it might hurt some, but as these guys all know, my balls are just not the sensitive type. I like life on the more 'rough and ready' side." And then looking directly toward Jim, he added, "And I don't mean just while diving."

And with that statement in the air, all of the other men in the pool, made comments such as, "Damn right man!" "You better believe it!" "Hell those balls are like baseballs and love to be hit!" And George added in, "From what I've seen and done to 'em myself, hell I don't think they got any feeling left in 'em at all!"

"Hey Jim. Reach over there and grab onto 'em." Mike suggested to Jim as Rawl moved up closer to them. "Grab 'em, and squeeze. He will love it, and I do mean love it! He likes his balls to be played with like using 'em for playing pool. He likes the feel of 'em getting hit on real quick and fast, just like hitting 'em with a pool cue."

Acting as though Rawl was completely in step with what Mike was suggesting, he did, in fact, move up, skin to skin close to Jim, grinned and slightly uttered, "Yeah, yeah."

Realizing that what he had just moments ago had secretly expressed to himself – that he knew he wanted 'to get close' to Rawl – he did reach out and place his hand under the soft velvety bag that was holding, what felt like, two golf balls. He had heard what had been said, and he knew Rawl had not objected to how they had talked about his balls, and how rough he liked to have them treated, so he did grab onto both balls with a strong force. He was now in the middle of three really hot guys – Mike, with his strong fingers that were attached to his massive arms, moving their way up and into his ass crack – Rawl, reaching over and placing his hand up and on his shoulder and slightly massaging his neck, as he kept uttering, "Yeah, yeah," as he was encouraging Jim to squeeze his nuts even tighter and tighter, and additionally Todd, who's right hand was strongly and forcefully, manhandling his balls, and grabbing onto the base of his dick. He was loving each and every feeling. He was in complete heaven. He was manhandling Rawl's balls and his dick – and his own balls and his dick, as well as his asshole – were being paid some very good and exciting attention. Attention that his body simply had never had before, and an opportunity to enjoy the feel of one magnificent body that was looking him in the eye, and silently, asking for, "More, yeah, more!"

Rawl looked at Jim's face and softly, yet forcefully said, "Yeah man, yeah! Roll 'em around some, yeah, now really grab 'em – really grab 'em, that's why they're there! Yeah man, yeah! I like that, I do, I really do! Yeah, tight man, tight! These other guys in here, they think getting their nuts grabbed onto really good and tight hurts, but to me man – that is what I like! It feels good! Yeah man, yeah! You are doing it – you're doing it! Hard, hard! Oh yeah man, thanks. Thanks! That just about makes my day!"

Slightly hugging onto Jim as he continued to place more and more finger length up into Jim's ass, Mike was taking advantage of knowing that Jim was rather consumed with playing with Rawl's bag and nuts, and he thus did take advantage of the situation and managed to fully finger fuck Jim's ass as completely as his index finger could go. Rawl knew what was happening back there, and he was enjoying being part of the four men, acting together, and enjoying the actions that were happening. He knew he was getting his bag squeezed and grabbed, exactly as he loved to have it done. He knew Mike was holding one big smile as he finger fucked Jim. And as part of the action, Todd was grabbing and squeezing the new dick and the bag of nuts that was now present, and of course, Jim was the man in the middle! He knew Jim was 'in heaven.'

Then looking over toward Todd, Rawl said, "Hey man! We've finally got ourselves a man in here that knows how to play. Where did you find this guy?"

Realizing that Rawl did not know the reality about Jim, and why Jim was renting the room, Todd then did finish telling Rawl about Jim being married and having children, and a little more detail about the new living situation.

He did include some additional information about what had happened already that day, and how the original agreement was – that there would be no funny playing around with Jim when there were gay guys around. But in addition, how that had all rather suddenly fallen apart – but with Jim's approval.

With 'that' rather now on the table, as a topic of conversation, Jim did relate to the others, rather briefly, about his prior experiences, and how he had been rather on the 'wanting to' side of things ever since he had gotten married. He admitted that what had happened so far that day, was really much more his fault than Todd's. He admitted that, "Yes, I asked for it. And right now I'm sure not sorry for doing it!"

With that statement out, Todd then asked, "Uh Jim, am I to assume then that playing around in front of you is O.K., and maybe even to the point that if someone wants to get you involved, that's acceptable too?"

"Oh hell yeah!" Jim replied with vitality. "Guys, let's face the facts here. A guy grows up, he keeps getting asked by friends and family, 'So when you gonna find yourself a girlfriend, settle down, and have some kids?' As young people we listen to others way too often and we don't stop and really listen to ourselves. Guys – that has been my life. I should have listened to myself and not listened to everybody else. My younger years and the things that happened back then, really were the true me, and instead of trying to change everything and make my life like all of my friends and family wanted, I should have looked at reality. Hey guys, today has been the pinnacle of the true me. This is the true life for me. I'm finally ready to be honest with myself. I have fought this off for way too long now. I am not being the true me, and I'm tired of it. The time has finally come to start being honest with myself. I know I've got some really bitchy times in front of me, but with your help guys, I'd like for this next year to be a big switching time for me. I've never really had any gay guys around, to rather lean on when I needed it, and if I may, I'd sure like to count each and every one of you as a main supporter while I change my life around. Can I maybe count on you guys as my helpers?"

With everybody pretty well crowded around in a rather tight group, one by one each of the men stated his commitment to helping Jim in any way he can. Todd then asked, "Uh Jim. Am I reading this right? Are you telling us that you are going to be leaving Barbara? Is that what you are saying?"

Now looking over at Todd, Jim replied, "Yeah Todd – yeah. The time has come. I've avoided my true feelings and thinking for way too long now, and hey, as fast as I acted with you today – within only minutes of me being in the house – finding out that you are a gay guy – and then almost forcing you to fuck me, plus having all of these hot hunks coming by today, and yeah – all good looking guys, all naked and bare, and my lusting and grabbing onto everything out there to grab onto – I now realize the time has come. I don't regret the things that happened to me in my younger years, I just regret that I did not follow through and accept just who I am, and start living that life. Now I start. Now I've got some buddies that are willing to help me whenever possible, so now I'm taking the step. Like I said, it's gonna be bitchy, and I know that, but I can't keep living a lie anymore."

– – – – – – – – –

"Hey Jim. A registered letter came for you today. I signed for it." Opening the letter, actually something that looked much more like a formal document, Jim replied, "Oh thanks. I really don't think I need to wonder just what this is. My last few weekends at home have not been what I would call the greatest, and I kinda figure, this is Barbara's formal statement of where we stand."

As Jim opened the envelope, which did have an attorney's name and address on the front of the envelope, Jim did say, "Yip! Sure enough. The divorce papers. I knew that, when you said a registered letter arrived. This year has been a struggle, and I told all of you guys the first day I was here that I knew it was gonna be, but now it's all coming to an end."

"Uh, Jim – you O.K.? I knew this day was gonna happen sooner or later, but now that it's here, how are you?"

"Well – not so sure – I guess. Feeling free and kinda in my own control, but then, ya gotta remember, I'm not gonna be as close to the kids as I'd like, but that's what happens when big changes occur. That part hurts. I think Barbara will be pretty good in letting me see the kids as much as I can, and she's a smart enough gal to really understand just why everything is like it is. Like I've told you in the past, I really do think maybe she kinda knew – in her heart – that this was gonna happen sometime, she just did not know when or how soon. Our last few months, well since about Christmas time, things of course kept getting a little more tense around each other, and then, like I told you after I got back from the Easter weekend, she just up and asked me if I wanted a divorce, and I told her about me kinda starting to realize the true me and, thankfully, she and I did manager to have an adult conversation about how to work on stuff. Of course our main concern was the kids."

"What'd you tell her about how you started really finding out?"

"I just told her that I had met some guys here in town, and when I met them and started having some beers with them once in awhile, that was really giving me the first strong signals that I really was trying to live the wrong life, and once I started spending more and more time together with them, the more convinced I was that – yes – I really am a gay man, and I was living the wrong life."

"How'd she handle that?"

"I think, about as strongly as any person could, when they are being told that their entire life is about to change from what they had expected."

"Well, what happened after that conversation – I mean – like as to sex?"

"It stopped! Everything changed, and I started sleeping in the extra bedroom, and after that weekend, my trips home really were more to see the kids, and then of course some more of the, 'how are we gonna handle this,' conversation."

Holding up the divorce papers, Jim looked at Todd and simply said, "It's just one more step in one big bad situation. I should have known, before I got married, that I was more anxious to be with guys than I was to be with some gal – Barbara included – but then, we try to do what all of our friends and family expect us to do, and sometimes it is the wrong thing. So once you make the wrong choices – in other words – let other people tell you how to live your life, you gotta go through all of the changes that you gotta go through. I still feel bad for Peggie and Tommy though. Being little kids, they just are not grown up enough to understand just why Mommy and Daddy are not living together, like they're supposed to, and used to. The kids always think they are the ones that caused the problems."

"So what's up next, Jim? Now what? Do you know?"

"Yeah, I guess I do. Rawl and I have had a lot of conversations over this little situation lately, and we both knew that it was gonna happen pretty soon, and so as soon as I can tell him the envelope arrived today, then our next step is looking for an apartment. We didn't want to do anything until the divorce papers had been filed – so that nobody could point a finger at him as being the reason – so now we can make our next move, and start looking at the long run, and having each other as our own. And so, as I know you've damn well known for the past few months, as soon as Rawl and I find our place, you are loosing a roommate."

"Well yeah, gotta admit, that is no news to me. Even without us talking about it directly, the way you two have been spending your time and energy together – ever since that very first day when you two met – it's no surprise to me. Sure am gonna be sorry you're not gonna be around here as much, but then let's face it – you've spent a hell of a lot more time over at Rawl's place than you have here, lately. I know, and I don't blame you any. I know both of you guys have a lot in common, and not the least of which is your ways of playing in bed. Both of you guys like it rough and tough, and that started the very first day you were here and met each other. And of course, when you saw that swinger he's got hanging down there with those golf balls – all packed up nice and neat – that was the final selling point."

Grinning rather broadly at Todd, Jim responded, "Yeah, I like that swinger that hangs down there, but I gotta be honest and tell you that I like it a whole lot more when it ain't swinging – but rather standing up, and saluting. And when that thing stands up and salutes, it looks like the whole Army brigade is standing at attention."

"You know Jim, you and Rawl do make a very handsome couple

together, and I am so damn glad that you've got him to be with you – especially, now, when this night arrived – and is gonna be with you while this whole divorce thing is happening, and I know way, way, beyond that."

"Me too! I'm a hell of a lot more thankful that I've got him than you are – let me tell you. He is truly my man. There is no way that I could have ever thought, on that Sunday morning, when I stopped here to ask about renting a room, that my life was gonna take such a radical and pleasant change. And finding Rawl, and having Rawl, is a big part of that change. I thought that when this night finally came – when this arrived – I was gonna take him out to dinner and tell him the news over a really fine dinner – as if I was proposing to him. But sorry, I just cannot hold it any longer. I've gotta tell him, and I've gotta tell him as fast as I can! I've gotta give him a call, right now, and tell him – 'It's finally here man! It's finally here!' "

About the Author

Wade Wright is an older gay man, now partly, or fully retired, *depending on the circumstances at the time*, living in Arizona as he has for the past fifty years. Grandfather of four, and the survivor of two sadly shortened gay relationships!

Wade Wright is also the author of:

Family Matters: And Sometimes, It Just Does Not Matter
Totally Unexpected
The Carpet Installer
Jay, Jake and Jimmy
In Cemetery Park
Marshmallow Cream – And Some Hard Pieces of Chocolate
"Yes Cops Do It, - Oh Yeah!"
The Two Straight Guys
Apartment 117
Married Men On The Loose
We Have Just Landed – Vol. 1 and Vol.2
The Four B's: Big, Bold, Black and Beautiful